CARLETON'S MEADOW

**Center Point
Large Print**

**This Large Print Book carries the
Seal of Approval of N.A.V.H.**

ॐ श्री गणेशाय नमः

LAURAN PAINE

CARLETON'S MEADOW

CENTER POINT PUBLISHING
THORNDIKE, MAINE

This Center Point Large Print edition
is published in the year 2002 by arrangement with
Golden West Literary Agency.

The text of this Large Print edition is unabridged.
In other aspects, this book may vary from the original
edition. Printed in Thailand. Set in 16-point
Times New Roman type by Bill Coskrey.

ISBN 1-58547-098-8

Cataloging-in-Publication data is available from the Library of Congress.

ONE

ARRIVAL OF A STRANGER

A MAN could insulate himself against the cold, and against rainfall, and perhaps with less success he could also devise protection against wind, and, as the hunched-up horseman told his horse in a gravelly voice, if a man had a lick of sense, he'd only travel when the weather was good, when the sun was shining, when there was grass up to his stirrups, and the nights were warm, then he wouldn't have to contend with any of those other damned things, like wind and rainfall and cold.

Of course, if a man was going to travel any distance at all, and if he planned on doing it a-horseback, why then just about inevitably he was going to encounter weather changes. Horseback travelling was slower than going by stage, especially if the horseback-traveller did not follow the roads. The weather changed every few months. It usually went from tolerable to intolerable. If the rider were heading towards the southwestern desert country, then even the summertime was intolerable.

But, as the hunched-up rider also told his horse, it wasn't always possible to pick the times of year when a man travelled, or, even had that been possible, it was seldom possible to pick his time of arrival.

But it wasn't rainfall nor cold nor wind that had the horseman swearing and peering from beneath his tugged-down hatbrim. A man could usually make his way throughout those natural calamities, bitter though he felt towards them.

It was fog.

Most rangemen were either born with, or somehow acquired, an infallible sense of direction. But in strange country they required something to sight on; a mountaintop, or a river, or the place where the sun rose and set. Instinctively, when the rider topped out up north two days earlier, he had put his faith in a round, thick mountain which had, at that time, been on his left, which was westerly. For two days he'd done right well, climbing over low hills and crossing open stretches of grassy meadows.

Then he had awakened this particular morning in a fog so thick it had taken him half an hour just to locate his hobbled horse, and afterwards, when he'd saddled up and turned southward, it had been like riding across the bottom of a very dirty dishpan, with the soapy water still in it.

The fat mountain would still be on his left. He knew enough to hold his horse's ears due southward. But after three hours he began to have an uneasy feeling that he was no longer travelling southward. There was nothing to verify this feeling, except something deep down inside which didn't tell him which way he *was* going, it only told him that he'd strayed a few degrees, over the past few hours, and now was not holding due southward.

If he'd known the country there might have been some way to get re-orientated, but he'd never been in northern New Mexico before in all his forty years. He was a northern rangeman. He knew all the country between the Canadian line and the Devil's Postpile country of southern Colorado, and all the land running east and west from Idaho Falls to Nebraska's Omaha Indian country. But none of that helped one damned bit in the New Mexico fog.

Another thing that annoyed him, and about which he bitterly complained to the powerful big bay horse, was that of all the tales and anecdotes he'd heard in at least three dozen bunkhouses of the north country, not once had anyone mentioned fog in New Mexico. They'd mentioned summer heat so bad a man could fry his eggs on a flat rock before ten o'clock in the morning. They'd also mentioned rattlesnakes as thick through as a man's arm, spiders as big as a man's fist, and Mexican horsethieves who could out-Indian the best Apache when it came to stealth and slyness, but not a one of those story-tellers had ever said a word about fog.

His horse did not seem to mind very much. He plodded along exactly as he'd been doing now for two months, up hills, across bountiful, grassy meadows, through spits of spindly pines, through stands of smelly junipers and back and forth through boulder-fields of round rocks half as big as he was.

There was plenty to eat, his rider was thoughtful of the horse's welfare, he was well-shod, and whenever they had encountered some little cow town in the past, his rider had made straight-off, for the liverybarn where he'd had the horse hayed and grained and cuffed down good and hard.

The horse had seen lean times. He was seven years old and had belonged to the dark-eyed, burly man upon his back for four of those years. They had not always lived high on the hog, but the man worried more about the horse, by far, than the horse ever worried about the man, which was about the way things were supposed to be.

Fog was better, to the horse, than cold rain. He actually rather liked walking along with nothing to distract him. What you couldn't see you certainly did not have to worry much about.

Also, the horse was accustomed to the dark-eyed man's grumblings. They had travelled together, just the pair of them, for a lot of miles. The horse understood the man's moods and what his sounds meant, just as well as the man understood the horse.

He walked ahead through the fog not the least bit concerned that they might be off course. It did not matter; wherever they ended up, come evening, they would find feed and a place to lie and roll. If the man did not share such simple needs, that was not the horse's concern.

The man turned up his collar, hunched deeper inside

his old blanket-coat against the clammy chill and the moisture, and stopped now and then to listen, but hell, he might just as well have been the only person left alive on the whole blasted planet for all he heard or saw. Anyway, the fog was not a conductor of sound. He could—and he warned the horse of this—ride smack-dab into the middle of a bronco Apache camp without either the Indians or the traveller knowing either were within five hundred miles of each other until they bumped noses.

That is not what he bumped into, though.

The horse probably sensed something, because, very subtly, the sounds of his steel shoes suddenly began coming back to him more quickly, as though they were being reflected off something solid up ahead. But the horse did not care in the least, and by the time the man felt something solid across their path up ahead, the horse had already decided, from the close-by scents, that they were no longer lost in a sea of impenetrable grey.

The old building loomed up like a phantom structure, pitched roof slightly swaybacked, weathered old plank siding darker than the swirling fog which lay every-where, a tumble-down picket fence out front lying two-thirds hidden in an overgrowth of weeds and rank grass.

The man pulled up, the horse halted, the man let his gloved rein-hand drop slowly to the horn, and with his right hand, also gloved, he reached stealthily down to yank loose the thong which kept his sixgun from falling from its holster. He listened. There was not a sound. The feeling of this place was of desertion, abandonment. If there had been horses around they would have caught the scent and nickered. A dog would have barked, if someone lived in the ghostly old house. *Some*thing, anyway, would have made noise, chickens, a milk cow, even a man who might have heard him riding in.

There was the clammy, wet thick fog, and the silence, nothing else. He sat a long while with the small hairs along the nape of his neck stiffly erect, then he swung down and walked carefully left and right looking for a place to tie the horse. What he eventually came upon was an old, unkempt, blighted big apple tree. He left the horse over there and unbuttoned the blanket-coat so that if he had to, he could sweep it aside in one movement and draw the gun.

He could have called out, but he knew better. Instead, he fixed the location of the apple tree in mind, then he slowly explored the yard. Once, he cracked his shin by stepping upon a hand-rake some idiot had left lying in the grass, tine-side up. The moment his boot touched it, the thing jumped up and its broken handle struck hard across his lower leg. He swore, flung the old rake away, rubbed his shin, then, a hundred feet farther along, he came upon the cathedral-like big massive phantom-barn. It looked more ghostly than the old house had looked, because it was larger, and also because, from his first sighting out a few yards, when the filmy fog slid past, the old log barn seemed to be exuding some eerie variety of cold smoke.

He went over there, found the door without difficulty, walked in and halted as soon as he was out of the fog.

The barn smelled deserted; it smelled dank and musty, not the way it should have smelled, of horses and leather, and hay in the loft.

He sighed, looked at the sagging old stall doors, at the abandoned pieces of broken harness hanging here and there upon whittled pegs, and decided that at least he and the big bay horse would hole up here until the blasted fog lifted.

He neglected to explore the barn. Understandably, he assumed it had been deserted for many years, and in fact he was correct. If it hadn't been it wouldn't have 'felt' like it did, nor would it have had that musty scent.

He turned to look back out into the yard. Visibility was limited to roughly twenty feet. He had of course experienced fog before, but not very often as thick as this fog was, nor as cloying—clammy and moist. He fished inside the blanket-coat for his tobacco, and went to work rolling a smoke. He had both hands busily occupied at this chore when he felt the very gentle pressure in his back.

He stopped work on the cigarette. In fact, he almost stopped breathing too. He had heard nothing, not even a hint of a sound. He was not a superstitious man; at least he had scoffed at the superstition of others most of his life, but right at this particular moment, blinded by smoke-like greyness, in a country he knew absolutely nothing about, absolutely lost, and feeling that pressure only very gently, he was ready to believe anything at all.

Then the earth-bound voice spoke behind him.

"Keep your hands in front. Don't move and don't make a sound."

He felt his holster being emptied, but he was almost relieved to discover that, whoever he was, he was just as much flesh and bone as any other human being. In answer to the man whose gun was in his back he said, "Mind if I finish rolling this smoke?"

The man back there seemed to hesitate before he finally answered. "Go right ahead. You can even light it."

The dark-eyed man did those things. He inhaled, exhaled, let go with a big ragged sigh, then said, "Mister, if you're not a ghost, you got to be in as bad a situation as I'm in. I never in my life been in such a lousy country before."

The man with the gun hesitated once more, before speaking. "Pull out the badge and toss it back here."

The dark-eyed man stiffened. "Badge? What badge? What the hell are you talking about?"

The next moment a tremendous flash of blinding heat swept over him. He did not even feel himself falling.

TWO
THE OUTLAW

THE FOG hung on hour after hour. Once, a wolf howled nearby, and although the sound came mutedly to the pair of men inside the old log barn, as though, perhaps the wolf were a long distance off, he could not have been very far or his sounding would never have reached the men. He more than likely was just on the outskirts of the ghostly old ranch buildings.

There was no danger. Wolves had exceptionally keen noses. Even if the wolf had a den among the abandoned buildings, by now he had detected the man-scent and that would keep him away for a very long while. Possibly he would never return at all.

The younger of the two men inside the old barn had made a small cooking fire inside a horse-stall. It was a very unique place to build a fire. In fact, there was not a living stockman who wouldn't have been highly indignant about something like that, even in an old abandoned barn. It was ingrained into stockmen from earliest childhood never to have any kind of a fire near a barn.

The younger man had cleared the ground before bringing in his faggots and creating the fire. He had also brought in the bay horse tied to the apple tree, off-saddled him and turned him into a stall across the way, beside the stall holding the younger man's own black gelding.

Then the younger man had rummaged the saddlebags and blanketroll of the man he had knocked unconscious, exactly as he had done with the older man's jacket after knocking the older man senseless.

He did not say much even when he watched his victim beginning to stir, and later, even when he'd rassled them up something to eat and had afterwards sat back watching the older man, whose ankles were tightly tied, drink his black java and roll his after-supper smoke.

He made a kind of an apology though, when the older man had first come around, had sat up gingerly feeling the back of his head where only his crushed-down hat had saved him from having his scalp lacerated.

"I thought you were lying," he told the older man. "Otherwise maybe I wouldn't have busted you over the head."

There was actually no headache, but there *was* a neck ache, which the older man did not attempt to explain to himself as he concentrated in cold fury upon his assailant.

What he saw was a lean, angular, wide-shouldered rangerider, perhaps in his late twenties or early thirties, who wore a Colt with ivory handles, and enough silver on his belt-buckle and spurs to indicate the younger man was a Southwesterner. He guessed the younger man was an outlaw. He had a small lump on the back of his head to support this notion, but right at the moment he was far too indignant to care about anything except freeing his ankles so that he could extract payment in full for being struck down from behind. Even when the younger man said, "I brought in your horse and looked after him," the older man was not even a little bit mollified. He had always considered any attack from the rear as cowardice. He still did. After lighting the cigarette he stared across their small fire and said, "Sonny, you just take the belt off my ankles."

The younger man smiled, and wanly waggled his head. "You carry a grudge, and that's not a good way to be, Mister. I told you—I really figured you were a lawman."

"Well, what the hell's so bad about being a lawman that you got to hit them over the head from behind?" demanded the older man. "Unless of course you're one of those fellers who goes around stealing other folk's money, or maybe their horses and cattle."

The younger man sat in the flickering firelight studying his companion for a while, without replying. Eventually he said, "We're neither of us going anywhere until the fog lifts, which could be a couple of days. We got no cards to kill time with, Mister, so I'm going to tell you a story. . . . My name is John Barron. Folks always called me Jack, the same as they called my father Jack when his name was the same—John Barron."

The older man smoked, and leaned in relative comfort,

and studied the hard, weathered, youthful face across from him. He'd seen a hundred just like that young, raw-boned rangeman, had in fact spent most of his life among them.

"This here barn you're sitting in," went on John Barron, "was built by my father, when I was a button. Him and my mother are buried yonder a short piece. When the fog lifts you'll see the log fence around their burial ground. I come back here every couple of years and make sure the fence is still up, and no varmints been at the graves.

"I was born in that house you bumped into. That was almost thirty years back, Mister. My folks came across from Missouri in a wagon. They staked out this land, set up the buildings, and when they weren't holding off Mex marauders or In'ians, they put together a little herd and planted a big garden, and raised a few head of horses."

The older rangeman had heard this same story, with regional variations, five hundred times. "Then the In'ians came one night," he said, exhaling smoke, then leaning to drop the stub of his cigarette into their little fire.

Jack Barron said, "Nope. You've heard it before. We all have. But this time it wasn't In'ians, it was a free-grazer by the name of Leo Cantrell."

The older man nodded. He'd also heard this variation. "How old was you?"

Jack Barron answered quietly. "Too damned young, Mister. 'Way too damned young. And by the time I was big enough to hold a gun, they'd run down this Leo Cantrell over near Las Cruces, and hanged him for murder."

The older man sighed. "That ended it, sonny."

Jack Barron considered the hard, square-jawed face opposite him. "Not that easy," he said.

"You can't shoot a ghost," stated the older man.

Jack Barron's answer was softly said, "That's right. Did you ever hear the name Len Cantrell?"

The older rider hadn't. "Nope. But if he's local there'd be no reason for me to have heard the name. I never been in northern New Mexico before—and if you'll hand back my gun, sonny, and untie my legs, after I settle with you, I'll turn right round and head back the way I come, and never come back here again for as long as I live."

Jack Barron's sunk-set grey eyes kindled with a tough, appreciative ironic smile. "There's still some Cantrells," he explained, ignoring the older man's other statement. "I'll settle with them."

The older man leaned his shoulder against logs and gazed a little pensively at this companion. After a while he said, "That's downright foolish. How old is this Len Cantrell?"

"A few years younger'n I am," replied Barron. "All I know for a fact is that when they hung Leo Cantrell over near Las Cruces, he had his woman and kid living in a free-grazer's wagon-camp over there."

The older man sat a long while gazing across the fire in quiet silence, but eventually he said, "I'll tell you what I think, Jack. You got something wrong inside your head. If that free-grazer's kid is younger'n you, how can you hold him responsible for what his pappy did? Hell, he was even littler than you were, back in those days. For all you know he has as little use for his pappy as you have. You're figuring on killing someone you never met, don't know a damned thing about, and who's maybe as dead set against men like Leo Cantrell as you are."

Jack Barron slowly shook his head. "Mister, it runs a lot deeper than that. Those people outlawed me. Why do you think I was leery of you being a lawman?"

"How the hell would I know?" growled the older man. "I come riding into this damned place and got knocked over the head. That's all I know."

"Well, you damned well know an orphan kid in this kind of country has to shift for himself, and that's not easy. I stole a horse so's I could hire out riding. I was twelve years old and they caught me. But I escaped. When I was fourteen I raided a stage down near the Mex border. That time they *didn't* catch me . . . Mister, I never left the country because I had this settling-up to do. Since those days I've come a long way. They've got a price of two thousand dollars on my scalp."

The older man went silent again, sitting over there eyeing his captor, his square-jawed face tough-set in disapproval. Then he blew out a big, ragged sigh and spoke again. "You know what I think, Jack? I think you're a damned fool . . . Now don't give me that hard look, until I've had my say, then, if you want, you just untie my legs and we'll settle our own little score, with or without the guns . . . You've spent all those good years of your life trying to prove how mean you are. I don't believe you wanted those Cantrells that bad, or you wouldn't have waited this damned long. I think you just wanted to show the world how tough you were. All right; you've showed 'em. And they put a price on your topknot. I think you *like* being an outlaw. Hell, sonny, if I wanted a piece of someone's hide for a killing that happened twenty years ago, I'd have got that settled up with long ago—and so would you, I think. Jack, you got some pretty mixed up feelings inside you . . . Now, I've had my say. You want to untie me?"

The younger man sat like stone, until he eventually leaned and poked in their little fire with a faggot, which he afterwards pitched across the flames. He looked to be the older man's match, but that was one of those things no one could really be sure about until there'd been a show-down. After a while he picked up the tin pan, re-filled his cup with black coffee, and put the pan aside as he raised the dented cup and drank from it, looking across at the older man.

When next he spoke he said, "What's your name?"

The older man answered curtly. "Clay Anderson."

That did not mean anything. It was probably the older rangeman's true name, but it still meant nothing. Names meant a lot less than deeds, in the range country.

"Where you from, Clay Anderson?"

"Montana, mostly, but also Wyoming, Colorado, Idaho and Nebraska. I never been south before." The older man grimaced. "I'd ought to have my brains examined for getting the notion there might be something worthwhile down here, too . . . Fog—then you." Clay Anderson shook his head slowly. "I'll tell you something, Jack. Where I come from we've got hundreds of 'breed In'ians got more to be bitter about than you'll ever have—and they managed to grow up as *men*." Clay Anderson's forthright manner had exacerbated a lot of men, in his time, and he had the scars to prove it, but he had never made any attempt to change his nature. He did not temporise now, either. "Saddle up, when this damned fog lifts, and go over where this feller's son is, and shoot him, and you know what that'll do for you? Not one damned thing. But if you got any conscience at all, and if you're lucky enough not to get shot one of these days, you'll end up a saloon-drunk with a whole raft of ghosts haunting you."

Jack said, "You should have been a preacher," and finished his coffee.

Clay leaned to refill his tin cup, which emptied their pan of hot coffee. He cupped the container between work-scarred hands for the pleasant warmth, and continued to gaze across the fire. He had no more to say.

Outside, the dense fog hung low and thickly damp, like cold, wet smoke. It did not seem to be lifting and it certainly was not being diluted with the passage of time. Across the barn's wide runway the horses drowsed, occasionally chewing old hay from the loft, which was not very palatable, but it was better than a snowbank.

The fire kept things warm where the two men sat. It also provided enough light. Otherwise, it could have been high noon or late evening for all a man could tell by looking outside.

There was enough food to last them several days. Jack Barron had stock-piled his own supplies with what he had looted from Anderson's saddlebags. Except for the hostility between the pair of them, they could have sat out the bad weather quite comfortably.

As for company, there was very little chance that anyone else would ride in. Not in weather like they were experiencing. To appear, riders would need a strong motive.

That left them nothing to do but sit, keep the fire going, and wait. Clay Anderson also slept a little, dozing off in the comfortable warmth, propped with his thick shoulders against the barn's log back-wall. He had learned all he wanted to know about the man who had captured him. In fact, he now knew *more* than he cared to know. He was not a very complicated human being. He did not quite view things as being all wrong or all right, but neither did he have patience with men like his captor. He'd heard all kinds of excuses in his lifetime; usually they did not make one damned bit more good sense than Jack Barron's excuses made. He was disgusted. Not entirely with Jack Barron, but also with himself for being bushwhacked so easily. Fog or no fog, he should never have turned his back and he knew it.

He was forty years old. He had seen just about all there was to see, one way or another, or he'd heard about it. The only excuse he had was that he'd been a stranger in a new place—and careless—which was a pretty damned poor excuse.

From time to time he eyed his captor, sitting hunched across their little fire, and felt like swearing.

At himself.

THREE

SURPRISE!

THE OUTLAW took no chances when the grey fog began turning dark, as though it were a form of moist soot. He used his lariat to secure the arms of his prisoner behind Anderson's back.

Protest would have done no good, so the older man stoically succumbed. It made sleeping pretty damned awkward, and each time he'd awaken in the long, dank night, he'd glance over and see Jack Barron sitting there, blanket round his shoulders, like a slump-shouldered old buck-Indian. Maybe Barron slept, but Clay Anderson never saw him at it.

When morning came Barron was gone when Clay Anderson opened his eyes. For a moment the older man was hopeful, then he heard Jack talking to their horses over across the barn.

Later, when the outlaw was cooking breakfast, he said, "That's a mighty fine animal you've got."

Anderson's reaction was to show suspicion. "I paid good money for him, Jack, and I'm partial to him."

Little more was said between them for a long while. Jack untied Clay's arms and they ate in silence. Anderson's disgust over the lingering fog eventually prompted him to grumble. "I never saw fog lie in like this. Not even in the valley of Montana, where we get our share in the late autumn and winter."

Jack, who was either resigned to it, or accustomed to the fog, simply shrugged and finished his meal, then picked up his dented tin cup and savoured the bitter, black coffee. "You know how much money I got off that stage I robbed?" he asked, as though they had been discussing his depredations, which they hadn't. "Four hundred dollars. Hell, I always thought bullion coaches carried thousands."

"How did you know it was a bullion coach?" asked Clay.

Jack half-smiled. "I worked in the town and made a

study of the schedules and cargoes." He seemed pleased about this, but Clay made a deflating remark.

"Too bad you didn't keep on doing honest work."

Jack's smile faded but he kept gazing over at the older man. It was exasperating, being cooped up with someone who missed no opportunity to make a man look bad. "You never did anything dishonest," he growled, and Clay, head lowered while he fashioned his after-meal smoke, did not even raise his eyes when he replied to that.

"Yeah. I did. When I was a lot younger. Before I grew up in the head." He lit the cigarette, and finally gazed across the little fire. "But that don't make it right, and it sure as hell don't make it right for *you*."

Clay kept his head raised when he finished speaking. For a while the outlaw glared, then he lowered his eyes and stirred the fire a little but Clay did not relax. He did not draw on the cigarette either. After a long time he leaned slightly to speak quietly.

"You told me yesterday that you come back here every once in a while to tend the graves of your folks."

"What of it?"

"Well—I been listening to something, and it crossed m'mind that if there are cowmen hereabouts, or maybe townsmen if there's a town, and any of them pass by this old ranch and notice the graves get tended to regularly— knowing you lived here once and that there's a price on your head . . ." Clay blew smoke into the damp air and sat very still again, listening.

Jack Barron was like stone, but only until he understood the implications, then he flung off the old blanket draped round his shoulders, reached to yank loose the sixgun tie-down, and almost whispered when he said, "What did you hear? I don't hear anything. Are you sure?"

Clay was sure, but he delayed replying for a moment. "I'm sure. Now, it comes to m'mind that maybe the smell of wood-smoke travels farther in the fog than a man might think. That, or else they saw you, maybe, and trailed you. If they know the country the fog might not give them the kind of trouble it gave me."

Without a sound Jack unwound up off the ground, stepped to the stall door, leaned to peer both ways, then came back and swiftly stamped out their little fire. The next thing he did was palm his ivory-butted Colt and step back out into the runway of the barn.

"Out front," whispered Clay.

The moment Jack moved off, up towards the front of the barn, Clay Anderson leaned and swiftly pulled loose the belt binding his ankles. He arose, a trifle stiffly, moved across into the darker shadows of the stall near the door, and put on his roper's gloves. Whatever Jack had done with his sixgun, was anyone's guess, but Clay Anderson wouldn't have used it if he'd had the thing.

Jack came back, his footfalls a light whisper of leather over hard earth. Clay did not wait, he gauged the outlaw's nearness by his foot-sounds, then came out of the shadow-layers like a two hundred pound shadow and struck Jack Barron head-on. The outlaw's sixgun flew high and skidded away in the gloom.

It was not much of an encounter, Jack hadn't expected anything at all. Clay's impetus carried him ahead to a jarring hard impact, and although Jack realised what was happening within seconds, the older man did not let up.

Jack almost fell, in fact he went down on one knee, but immediately sprang erect. He was as quick as a cat and more than ten years younger. Also, he had that raw-boned, spare build that meant endurance. What he lacked, though, was the solid, devastating power of the older man. It was a brief contest between a sapling and a seasoned oak.

Clay never relinquished the initiative once he jumped forth from the stall. His gloved fists were like iron. He allowed Jack Barron to spring back upright, then he blasted him over the heart with a solid right hand, twisting his full weight in behind that blow, then he pressed in fast and crossed over with a stinging left, which lacked the right's power, but which was adequate to drive Jack back a step, just far enough for that sledging right to come up and explode like a cannonball alongside the younger man's jaw.

Jack went down in a heap, groped briefly with searching, numb hands, then fell forward flat out.

Clay leaned to make certain, then straightened back,

peeled off his gloves, shoved them under his bullet-belt, and flexed his knuckles. Even buckskin gloves were not much protection really, when a man was hitting something as hard as he could.

Clay found the fancy gun with the ivory-grips, dropped it into his own holster, kneaded his sore right hand and stood looking around. Having reversed things did not change *everything*. He was still at the bottom of a very dirty fishbowl unable to see a hundred feet in any direction, and totally lost in an alien place, but at least he was armed again, and whatever he now did was bound to be an improvement.

He did exactly the same thing Jack had done to him. He yanked off the outlaw's trouser-belt, lashed his ankles with it, then he went after the outlaw's lariat and bound the unconscious man's hands behind his back.

Finally, having caught his breath and with the pain in his right hand turning to a slow ache, something which he was accustomed to, somewhere in his body, being a man who worked hard and physically, he let go with a long sigh.

Now, he was free again, but in this instance freedom did not mean what it usually meant to an unattached man; he was still lost, still blind as a bat for all practical reasons, and now also, he was saddled with a damned renegade.

There was probably a town somewhere around. Finding it was something else. He wasn't altogether certain he wanted to find a town, anyway. All he wanted to do was turn north and head back the way he had come.

His ultimate decision was to do exactly that. Head north, and if he didn't out-ride the damned fog, at least he'd go *somewhere,* he'd fetch up in some other place which certainly could not be as unpleasant as *this* place was.

He went over, took down his saddlebags, returned to the stall and proceeded to fill them with what remained of the food, taking Jack Barron's coffee, salt and sugar, too.

After that, he went to lead out his bay horse, tied him, and re-secured the saddlebags before moving in to rig out his horse. He had his back to the front of the old barn, beyond which the fog was monotonously swirling like a grey pea-soup, bone-chilling without being actually very cold.

He saw nothing, never even turned to look back from his work as the four converging ghostly dark shapes seemed to float inward from different directions, faceless, rather formless, but purposefully moving closer until all four of them were blocking the wide doorless big opening.

All four strangers saw him in there, and after trading looks, moved soundlessly across the threshold and came towards him.

The bay horse suddenly threw up his head and turned to stare. It was too late, but Clay abruptly sensed other presences and also turned. He was facing four men with pulled-low hats, coats buttoned to their throats, gloved hands holding cocked guns, and deaths-head faces murkily discernible in the damp gloom.

One of the men said, "Left-handed now; lift out the gun and let it drop."

Clay's surprise passed. A quick sense of peril superseded it. He obeyed, disarming himself slowly and properly. Not even Wild Bill Hickok would have tried to draw against that kind of a full house.

One of the strangers gave a little grunt and pointed. "Who the hell's *that?* He was supposed to be alone."

It wasn't much of a distraction, but the astonished man knelt down and flopped the unconscious outlaw over onto his back, looked intently for a moment, then blurted out his words.

"Gawddammit, *this* is Barron."

The other three men flicked glances from Clay to the lumpy, slack shape tied with a lariat at their feet. One of them a dark, bearded man, said, "Mister, you was in bad company."

Clay agreed. "Yeah. That's a fact. I got lost in the lousy fog, rode in here, and this feller knocked me over the head. That was yesterday. I never got a chance to get him off guard until this morning."

The bearded man thought about this, then said. "Take off your hat. Ed, look and see if he's been hit."

One of the men stepped around behind Clay, looked,

then spoke. "Sure got a lump, Sheriff." Ed then went back beside the bearded man, gun slack in his fist, but still pointing at Anderson. "Maybe he's telling the truth."

The bearded man swore under his breath and stepped past to lean and stare at the unconscious outlaw. While he was doing this, Clay shook his head. He hadn't heard any sounds; that had been his ruse to get rid of Jack long enough to untie his legs and get set for the assault. But hell, there really had been men out there.

This was the most confusing damned country a man could ever wake up and find himself in.

One of the armed men moved around Clay and looked over the partially rigged out bay horse. Then he went further and leaned to look in at the stalled black horse. As he finished this inspection, he turned back, saying, "Sheriff, Barron's black's in a stall over here. His saddle's hanging in there too."

The bearded man slowly holstered his weapon and faced Clay Anderson. He did not look friendly or convinced. "What's your name, where you from, and what are you doing here?"

Clay answered each part of the question succinctly. Afterwards, he watched two of the men untie Jack Barron and hoist him to his feet, then slap his face to expedite recovery. It seemed to help. The outlaw tried to turn his head to escape the stinging light blows, and he also shuffled his feet to hold his balance.

The cowboy called Ed picked up the lariat, coiled it, and looked at the bearded lawman. When their eyes met Ed pointed upwards with a gloved hand to a massive old hand-squared barn baulk. "That'll do as well as any tree, Sheriff."

Clay stiffened in surprise. The lawman slowly unbuttoned his coat, shoved back his hat, then just as slowly nodded his head as he proceeded to pull off his gloves.

"You could haul a horse up, on that thing," he said, very calmly and matter-of-factly. "Pitch it up, Ed."

The lariat sailed up, and over, and came down the far side of the baulk. Clay was incredulous. "What the hell are you doing?" he exclaimed.

The lawman's bearded, strong face came down and around. He studied Clay a moment before replying in that same calm, matter-of-fact voice. "What's it look like we're doing, cowboy? We're fixing to carry out the law. That's what we're doing." He stood a moment, watching Clay, then he made a little contemptuous gesture. "Finish saddling up, Mister, get on your horse and ride out. And Mister, don't turn back, because if you do, so help me, you'll be next. We got the right. We found you in the company of a fugitive, with no reason at all to believe you wasn't his partner; we got as much right to hang you as we got to hang Barron."

FOUR

THE FOG-WORLD

CLAY ANDERSON did not move. He stared steadily at the bearded man. Ultimately he said, "You're no lawman."

The bearded man lifted his coat aside to show the nickel badge on his right shirtfront, let the coat drop back without a word, and as his possemen crowded in to listen, he jerked a thick thumb over his shoulder. "Ride out. I'm not going to keep telling you that."

Jack Barron was leaning against a horse-stall. He did not look as though he comprehended. In fact, he looked sick.

The rangeman called Ed put aside the coiled rope and went purposefully towards the bay horse, his intention to finish saddling and bridling in order to expedite Clay's departure.

Clay heeded none of them but the man with the badge. "Hell; he's got a right to a trial."

"Not around here he ain't," stated one of the rangemen.

"A yeller dog's got that right," stated Clay. "I'm not saying he shouldn't maybe be punished, maybe even hung. What I'm saying is that he's got the right to . . ."

"You talk too much," snapped the bearded, husky lawman. "I'm not going to keep telling you, Mister. This don't any of it concern you. Now get on that damned bay horse and ride out."

There were still guns in their hands, and excepting Ed behind him, busy at the saddling, none of them were close enough. If he had a choice, it was impossible to see. Maybe they wouldn't shoot him, they probably wouldn't, but he had a feeling that men who would lynch someone might not be too reliable when it came to being unpleasant. He said, "All right, Mister. And the first town I come to, I'll send a telegram to the nearest U.S. Marshal."

One of the other rangemen, a grizzled, greying, weathered man with a gash for a mouth, spoke with a ring of resignation to his voice. "Whit, you should have waited."

The man meant, simply, that they shouldn't have told Clay what they were going to do, they should have seen him on his way, *then* got down to their lynching-bee.

Clay looked at this older man; a person who could make that kind of remark had deceit in him. Clay said, "You're as old as I am, Mister."

The lipless rangerider nodded. "All right. But what's that got to do with anything?"

Clay did not respond. If the rider didn't know what it had to do with their present situation, all the explaining under the sun—or in the fog—wasn't going to change his view.

Ed finished with the bay horse, turned and lightly

tapped Clay's arm. "He's all set, Mister." Ed was younger. He did not seem as hard as the other men seemed, but clearly, he was one of them and he believed in what they were going to do. He stepped past, returned to the area of his companions, and whatever chance Clay might have had to seize a hostage, slipped away.

The sheriff gestured. "Get aboard, Anderson. Remember what I said; don't look back and don't turn back."

Clay made his decision. He glanced where Jack Barron was leaning. Now, the outlaw was white to the eyes. He was again in full command of his faculties. He knew what impended. When their eyes met, Jack Barron looked back glassily. He did not seem to be pleading for help, he instead seemed too frightened to think straight.

"Go fetch another lariat," Clay told the lawman. "I'm not riding out there, and have *this* on my conscience. Go ahead, Sheriff, fetch another rope."

"Oh hell," growled the large cowboy beside the lawman, and started forward, big hands balled up and rising.

The bearded man said, "Hold it, damn it," and ordered the truculent cowboy back, then he coldly smiled straight at Clay. "Ed, do like the man says, go fetch us another lariat."

Even the grizzled rangeman stared. Ed did not move out of his tracks. "But you said he could go, Sheriff, you said for him to ride out. Hell; he hasn't done nothing."

"Get the gawddamned rope," snarled the lawman, angered by this challenge to his authority. "Do like I said, Ed."

The grizzled man growled. "Don't you do no such a thing, Ed." The older man looked stonily at the lawman. "Whit, I agreed that Barron needed it. We all did, when we agreed to come out with you from town. But you've already said this other feller's done nothing. You can't hang him just for *being* here."

The sheriff faced this growing opposition with an angry retort. "How do we know he hasn't done something; he was in this damned old barn with Jack Barron wasn't he?"

"Yeah," dryly replied the older rangeman. "After having knocked Barron out and trussed him up."

"Outlaws have fallings-out," snapped the sheriff, but he was losing ground fast and knew it.

The big cowboy, the one who had started for Clay, now sided with his companions against the sheriff. "Whit, what's wrong with just hauling them both to town for a trial? Barron'll get hanged sure as hell, anyway."

Now, finally, the sheriff made what to Clay Anderson was a revealing remark. "You don't know a damned thing about that, Turner. The law turned loose those Mexes I brought in didn't it? It'll sentence Barron to a couple of years in prison, and he'll be out again before you know it." The bearded man turned his hard, square face towards the older cowman. "Jess, for Chriz' sake, you of all people know what horsethieves and renegades deserve."

The older man, called Jess, did not relent, although he answered a little differently from the way he'd spoken before. "Whit, it's not Jack Barron I'm talking about. It's this Clay Anderson feller."

"A lousy outlaw," snarled the lawman. "Look at him standing there. Don't tell me, Jess, I been in this business too long. I can *smell* 'em."

Jess said, "Well, *I* can't smell 'em, so let's quit this damned bickering, get them their horses and head back for town."

Clay had no illusions as the bearded lawman turned and slowly stared at him. Given just half a chance, on the ride to wherever their town was, that lawman called Whit would shoot both Clay and Jack Barron—and say afterwards that they were attempting to escape, and this thought gave Clay an idea.

Maybe this damned fog wasn't such an enemy after all.

Ed brought forth Jack Barron's black and rigged it out. He had some assistance from the grizzled rangeman, and while Ed seemed to have accepted the change in plans probably about as he accepted most things, without giving them much deep thought, the older man looked to Clay Anderson as though he could not quite shake off the moments of dispute that readily.

When they got the horses saddled, they led them over to the rear of the weathered, sag-roofed old abandoned house, where the other saddled animals were patiently standing.

As they mounted Jack had a chance to lean close to Clay and say, "That son of a bitch is Sheriff Whitney Mosely. He hates my guts."

There was no time for Clay to ask why that strong animosity existed. The grizzled rangeman poked his horse between them and frowned. "You fellers shut up and set up there straight."

The fog forced the riders to stay bunched up, for a while at least, until Ed loped out ahead, leaving Clay to speculate why he had been sent on.

The grizzled man called Jess remained between Clay and the fugitive, not saying a word and scarcely more than occasionally glancing at them on his left and right. He dug out a plug of Muleshoe, gnawed off a corner, pouched it into his leathery cheek, then leaned to expectorate. He was now set for a long ride, apparently.

Clay rolled a cigarette, lit it, and wondered if anyone had found his weapon, back there, or had picked up Barron's gun with the fancy handles. They must have, but he hadn't seen anyone do it.

He smoked, pulled down his old hat, turned up his jacket collar against the dampness, turned and saw Jack looking steadily at him. Clay gave his head the minutest of little nods, then jerked it backwards and to the right.

Jack seemed to understand. He sat straight in his saddle affecting a look of either dejection or resignation, and when Sheriff Mosely turned, Jack looked away from him.

Mosely said, "You're a lucky bastard, Barron."

Jack continued to look away.

Ed loomed ahead, ghost-like, sitting perfectly still and facing the oncoming riders as he said, "It's just as bad over by the road, Sheriff, I'd say it ain't getting any better, it's spreading and getting thicker."

Mosely made a fretful remark. "How long's the damned stuff going to hang on?"

Jess answered. "I've seen it like this plenty of times down the years. I've seen it hang in these here lowland places sometimes for as long as a week." Mosely turned suddenly towards Jack. "The year your maw died it was like this most of the late autumn. Old Doc Grady used to call it a miasma."

That was the only personal remark any of them made to the outlaw, and if it seemed strange that Jess would be that sociable towards Barron now, and a half hour earlier had been perfectly willing to hang him, it wasn't strange, not according to the usages of the range country.

Clay finished his smoke, smashed it out atop the saddlehorn, snugged his collar closer and tugged a little at both his gloves as he measured the distance between himself and the men on ahead, then slowly turned towards Jess with a comment.

"I sure never figured I'd be that close to hanging as I was back there, Mister, and if you asked me I'd tell you your sheriff . . ."

"Nobody asked you," snapped the cowman. "You had your chance, cowboy. You had every chance in the world, so don't go blaming Sheriff Mosely nor any of the rest of us because your tail's in a sling now."

Clay saw Jack Barron lean sideways, left hand silently moving towards Jess's hip-holster. Instinctively, Clay spoke again, a little more swiftly, to hold the rangeman's attention, although this was not at all what he'd had in mind when he'd gestured to Jack with his head, back a mile or so.

"My tail's not in any sling, Mister," he told Jess. "But yours came awfully damned close to being in one, at the barn."

Clay tightened the hold on his reins, settled a little deeper in the saddle, turned his heels inwards at the ready. Jess was snapping back at him when he saw Jack's hand make its final grab for Jess's sidearm.

Clay did not wait one more second. He spun his big bay, sank in the hooks, and the completely astonished animal jumped so suddenly and far that Clay had to lunge for the horn with his right hand, and cling to it as his horse lit down in a wild run on a southwesterly course.

Behind him someone yelled, and someone else fired a Colt. Clay heard the sound easily, and winced, but apparently the slug hadn't been sent in his direction. He turned, just once, to peer back over his shoulder. Jack was coming after him in a flinging rush, riding far down the off-side of his speeding black horse like one of those oldtime redskin side-riders, shooting at the suddenly stampeded possemen back there.

It happened so suddenly only Clay had really been prepared. Even Jack was slower in getting clear, but, as Clay had thought back at the barn, the fog which had been his enemy for several days now, had now become his only real ally. Within moments he could no longer see Sheriff Mosely and his possemen, which meant that they could no longer see him either, to shoot at him. Having never much favoured fogs, he gave whispered thanks for it now, as he continued to race along blindly through the thick, cloying greyness.

He saw Jack Barron, but the outlaw was unable to catch up, or perhaps he wasn't really trying, perhaps he was hanging back in the hope that Mosely or one of the other possemen would come charging out of the fog so Jack could empty a saddle.

Clay yelled. "Jack! Get up in your saddle and give that horse a chance!"

Barron obeyed, probably because he knew, finally, that the pursuit would be just as wary of charging into him as he was of having those men do that.

Now, the black horse caught up easily. In fact, he slowly widened the gap by leading them as his rider holstered the Colt he'd snatched from Jess's holster, paying almost no attention to where they were going.

Finally, Clay hauled down the bay to rest him. They had to be at least two miles from where they'd made their break. Even if the possemen could find them in the fog, they couldn't do it quickly, so Clay yelled at Jack to slack off, to blow his horse. As he came up to ride stirrup with the outlaw, Jack smiled at him.

"I didn't figure it'd be that easy," he said. "Mosely got off one round at me, and he missed by a country mile."

Clay looked back, then looked forward, ignoring his companion's comments to say, "Do you have the faintest damned idea where we *are?*"

Jack's smile broadened. In a casual tone he said, "Sure, you just follow me, oldtimer."

Clay turned. Oldtimer! But he rode along saying nothing. If they had any chance at all, it had to lie in the hands of his companion.

FIVE

CARLETON'S MEADOW

FROM THE frying pan into the fire. Clay was free again—until he reflected on this and came to the grudging conclusion that he was not one damned bit better off, and in fact he just might well be *worse* off.

He still had no gun. Jack had the only weapon between

them, exactly as he'd had it back in the old barn. To top that off, Clay was now just as much a fugitive as Barron was. He rubbed his stubbled jaw, considered the ears of his mount, and decided that he'd done it again, had pulled another stupid manoeuvre.

However, there was something in the back of his mind which had been there since the day before, and which had firmed up quite a bit during supper last night when he and the outlaw had argued. Right now, though, he did not dwell upon anything but his fresh situation, and no way he studied it did he come out looking very well.

They must have covered six or seven miles. The only thing that even slightly pleased Clay was that as they began climbing very gently, the fog appeared to be thinning out, and a mile or so farther along, they rode up onto a high plateau and could turn, sitting their saddles looking back, and see out over the top of the low-hanging fog for miles on end.

"Thick as soup," Clay said, rolling and lighting a smoke. "That stuff's not going to break up for days."

The lifelong experience of Jack Barron the outlaw who had been in this territory for so long, prompted him to make a suggestion about that. "Predicting fog is like predicting rain. You'll be wrong more than you'll be right." Then he raised his arm, twisted and pointed towards the uphill side of their big, handsome meadow. "There's an old shack up yonder. We might as well hole-up there until the morning." As he dropped his arm and turned, he also said, "Mosely won't find us before we head out again. Don't worry."

Clay wasn't worrying. At least he wasn't worrying about Sheriff Mosely, and whatever else he had to feel concerned about he kept to himself as they cut diagonally across the big, sunshiny meadow, which, in itself, was like being re-born into a brand new, wonderfully clean world, after those damp days in the fog.

It was all new country to Clay Anderson. He'd had a vague notion that all of New Mexico was desert. In fact he'd anticipated having to carry a canteen everywhere he went, and if his meandering hadn't been interrupted by this mess he was now in, after another couple of weeks of southerly riding he would have had to do just exactly that; he would by then have been far southward into the New Mexico desert, but the way things looked now, and the way he *felt* now, the New Mexicans could keep their damned desert—and all the rest of their territory as well, if he could just shake clear enough to head back where he'd come from.

As they crossed the huge grassy meadow it occurred to him that a place like this would run several hundred cows with their calves, and with enough bulls to keep them calvy most of the year, and yet, excepting some age-old rockhard droppings here and there, there was no sign of cattle or even horses up here. He finally yielded to curiosity and asked his outlaw-companion about that.

Jack's reply was matter-of-fact. "You see those

forested top-out up ahead of us? Well, there's been In'ians up there since anyone can remember. Folks just don't put livestock up here to feed a band of mangy redskins, and that's what's happened in the past when the cowmen, like Jess Smith, that posseman back at the barn, used to turn out herds up here."

Clay rode the balance of the distance across the lush meadow eyeing those westerly peaks and slopes, which were so heavily timbered it was doubtful whether the sun had touched the ground up there in centuries. In Montana, the cowmen wouldn't have allowed this kind of a situation to exist for very long. Then Clay shrugged and dropped his gaze to the hidden old log cabin they were approaching, as they worked in past the first ranks of giant old pines and firs.

He knew oldtime trapper-shacks when he saw them, but he'd never expected to find one this far south, and said as much when they dismounted out front and tied their horses in fragrant shade.

"Wasn't a trapper who built it," stated Jack Barron, then qualified his statement. "Well, he didn't *only* trap. He was just a feller who liked not having to be around folks. He came out from Missouri in the same wagon-train my folks were part of. My folks said he'd been a schoolteacher back east. Anyway, he came up here, made his cabin, and for some reason or other, the In'ians never attacked him. And that was back when there was fighting just about every month of the year."

Inside, there was a long wall-bunk, some shelves which were slowly disintegrating, a fir floor which was also rotting, but the roof, rafters, and walls of peeled fir logs, were as solid as the year they were emplaced.

Clay went to a bench, sat down, looked out the open door, and shook his head. "In the morning, you go your way and I'll go mine." He turned to watch the outlaw kneel, over near the ancient mud-wattle fireplace and lift aside a large flat rock. Barron pulled something from the underground hole and held it aloft. "Beans," he said proudly, "and tinned peas. I used to keep a couple of guns down in here too."

Clay arose, went over and peered into the hole. It had apparently been made of stone and mortar by the cabin's builder because it looked very old and much-used. As Clay turned back to his bench Jack replaced the rock, stood up and turned.

"All right, oldtimer, you go your way if you're a mind to. I'm not going to stop you. Not after the way you helped save my hide today."

Clay put a hostile look upon the younger man. "The next time you call me oldtimer I'm going to knock all your ribs loose."

Jack went to a slab-table, put aside his cans of food, tossed away his hat and leaned there, looking back towards Clay. "Come to think of it, you gave me a pretty good going-over at the barn this morning."

Clay was unimpressed and continued to sit and gaze

out the door. "You're alive, aren't you," he said, then arose to walk forth and care for his horse.

It took a little getting used to, all that delightful sunshine. It also did something to his spirit, because when he returned to the cabin and found the outlaw cooking a meal at the fireplace, he turned and went out back to fetch in a big armload of wood, which he dumped on the floor, then reported that he had almost fallen into a well-box out there someone had neglected to cover adequately.

Barron said, "Yeah; that was me, a few days back."

Clay frowned. "You spend time up here, then?"

Barron nodded. "Yeah. Every now and again."

Clay sighed. "Great. That's how the law nearly trapped you this morning. If they've been keeping watch for you, they likely know about this place too."

Barron was not very concerned. "Any horseman riding up here to Carleton's Meadow crosses one hell of a lot of open country before he even gets close to this house—and if I'm here, I see him. Even if I'm out in the forest somewhere, I see 'em coming." He turned. "You're sure jumpy."

That might have been the trouble. "Never been an outlaw before," stated Clay, putting aside his hat. "Never even been much of a fugitive from the redskins." He watched the rawboned, lanky younger man at the fireplace. "Which way is Las Cruces from here?" he asked, and Jack Barron slowly turned.

"What do you want to know that for? You been saying all along you can't wait to get the hell out of the territory."

"That's on the way out, isn't it?" asked Clay.

"Hell no. It's on the other side of these mountains, and southwesterly another fifty, sixty miles."

Clay pursed his lips. "You're a liar, did you know that, Jack? You told me you were just waiting to get to Las Cruces to kill that kid of Cantrell's. Now you're saying you've been over there."

"I didn't tell you any such a thing," exclaimed the outlaw.

Clay looked doubting. "You just told me where the town was. You wouldn't know that if you hadn't been there, most likely. And if you've been there, it was since your father was killed—which means you were in Las Cruces when Cantrell's kid was also there."

"Well; what of it! That was a long time ago and back then I hadn't made up my mind to kill him."

Clay pointed. "Stir those beans or we'll be eating charcoal." As the outlaw turned, and reached swiftly for his stirring-stick, Clay also said, "Tell me straight out, Jack, and don't lie: You stopped a coach and got four hundred dollars from it. And you stole someone's horse back when you were pretty young. What else have you done?"

Jack smiled. "That breedy black horse I ride—well—now you know why Whit Mosely hates my guts. I stole it right out of the liveryman's back corral down in Tiburon, right when Mosely was dealing to buy it."

Clay leaned with both elbows atop the old slab table eyeing his companion. After a while, when Jack was measuring in coffee to mix with the water in the pan, Clay said, "You're a pretty sorry outlaw, Jack. One coach and two stoled horses. Why hell, I've known fellers who did *that* much damage all in the same week." Clay arose, went to the door with his back to the room, and the glaring man at the fireplace, looked all around out there to satisfy himself they were, indeed, alone on Carleton's Meadow, then he turned back and serenely met the outlaw's glare.

"You know what I think?" he asked the outlaw.

"No, I don't know what you think," snapped the younger man, "and I don't want to know. You talk a lot, and you never have a whole lot to say."

Clay accepted the rebuke and returned to the table to watch Jack spoon his soggy beans and peas onto their tin plates, then, using the same stick, to stir their coffee before coming to the table and putting down the plates before filling the tin cups with his deadly coffee.

When he finally dropped down opposite Clay, he glared. "I'll be glad when you pull out, tomorrow, Anderson. You helped me today, but I'm doing you a favour too—I'm letting you go."

Clay could have answered that Jack had no alternative, unless he wanted to be continually harangued, which no man would have wanted, but all he actually did was to go to work on the beans and peas, and afterwards to walk outside to get a twisted swatch of curing grass to clean his plate with.

While he was out there, he made another long examination of their big valley. It seemed incredible to him that the whiskery-faced lawman wouldn't have guessed where Jack would head. He kept watching the eastern far side of the meadow expecting to see horsemen come up, over there, at any moment.

They did not come, not in what remained of the morning nor in the afternoon, and finally, when shadows advanced down the mountainside like ranks of ghostly soldiers, presaging evening, they still did not come. Maybe they thought the fog was up here on the big meadow too. Maybe—and Clay thought this more probable—they did not want to make the trip because of the Indians up higher along the rims and peaks.

But they would arrive the next day. Clay was just about convinced of that. Jack Barron couldn't be the only man in the countryside who knew fog did not reach up as high as Carleton's Meadow.

From what Clay had seen of that lawman with the whiskers, he had no illusions; Sheriff Whitney Mosely was not a man simply to accept the humiliation of having a pair of prisoners escape from his custody, philosophically.

Clay put out his last smoke of the day, watched his

hobbled bay horse out in the middle distance cropping good grass, then turned as Jack came along, and asked if those damned redskins up there ever came down and stole horses off Carleton's Meadow.

Barron made a crooked small smile. "Not mine," he replied, and left that enigmatic remark hanging between them as he went over to his saddle to pull loose his blanketroll before returning to the warmth of the old cabin, to unroll it near the embers of the dying fire.

Clay turned back to watching his bay horse with a little grimmer expression, and just before he also went after his blankets, he softly made an aloud comment.

"Not mine either, and if they do they'll sure as hell wish they hadn't."

Nightfall came slowly although the shadows were already in position hours ahead of deep dusk. Carleton's Meadow was a very peaceful, lovely place. It reminded Clay of some of the highland meadows of Montana and Wyoming—called 'parks' in the high-country.

The last thing he said to Barron before crawling in, was: "You recollect the name of the feller who built this cabin?"

"Yeah. Carleton. I think his first name was Henry, but I know for a fact his last handle was Carleton. Why; you wondering how the meadow got its name?"

"Yeah," stated Clay, and rolled up onto his side and closed his eyes.

SIX

A UNIQUE MEETING

CLAY WOULD long remember Carleton's Meadow. Not because anything noteworthy happened up there, but because, when he opened his eyes about three o'clock the following morning, he did so with a full-fledged idea already hatched in his mind.

He arose, and did all the things he had to do in his stocking feet. The last thing he did was pull on his boots. He did that outside in the cold early morning, as he turned to peer back inside at the snoring outlaw dimly discernible where the coals in the fireplace shed an eerie red glow across the small room.

Then he led his saddled horse a dozen yards before mounting up.

The blanketroll was not as neat as he ordinarily made it before lashing it behind the cantle, but it would not slip and that was the main consideration. Also, he was armed again, thanks to the involuntary loan of that sixgun Jack Barron had taken from the hard-eyed cowman back in the fogbank, and that was a very reassuring feeling to any rangeman, such as Clay Anderson, who rarely used guns but who had become so accustomed to wearing one that he felt undressed without a sidearm.

Now, he had to make his way across the mountains. That did not bother him very much even though he'd never seen those slopes until the previous day. For two reasons he headed his horse up through the forest without worry. The first consideration had to do with the fact that he was not trying to adhere to any particular schedule. All he had to know was that when Jack Barron took up his trail, Clay would be several hours ahead of him in a countryside where trailing would be difficult even for a redskin, and just about impossible for a white-skin.

His second reason for not worrying was because, without any fog to circumvent it, his native instincts would tell him where to go. He'd been riding through unknown territories most of his life, and so far he'd never got lost. The trees and slopes might be lost, but not Clay Anderson.

He would have preferred to have remained back there in the warm shack in his bedroll, but that, too, was something he had become just about immune to—comfort was a wonderful thing if a man could afford it, but if he'd never been able to do that, he just naturally thought, rather, in terms of the things which had to be done, not in terms of the things he would have preferred to do.

He smiled to himself as his horse sought, and located, an angling game trail up through the trees. He had left a curt note behind saying simply that he was going over to Las Cruces.

That was all. He had not said he was doing this to warn the Cantrells against Barron. Nor did he suggest that he might take their side in this trouble. All he'd said was that he was going over there. Jack could damned well think what he chose to think. But Clay Anderson, who'd been in and out of a lot of bunkhouses in his lifetime, and who knew rangemen inside and out, backwards and forwards, was fairly certain of the course Jack Barron would follow.

By the time there was a sickly grey shading to the eastward sky he and the bay horse had found an old pathway which was more than a game trail, although it had, like most trails, probably started out that way. It seemed that at one time this course had been rather extensively travelled; at least it was wide and brushed off and, like all worthwhile high-country trails, did not hurl itself directly at the slopes, but circuitously switched back and forth gaining altitude a foot at a time, in order that the animals using it—two-legged or four-legged—could do so without exhausting themselves. Maybe *animals* were dumb but Mother Nature surely wasn't, she knew exactly how to complement the sinew and muscles and lungs of mobile critters.

By the time the sun arose it had turned still colder on the mountainside, thanks to all those generations of untouched big trees which inhibited light as well as heat. The sky overhead gradually paled out, changing from the frailest pastels to the strong, early-morning glow of a fresh new day, and this helped somewhat, down in among the trees, to brighten the way for Clay and his bay horse.

He had never intended to make the top-outs, then descend on the far side. No rangeman did a thing like that unless he absolutely had to, or unless he did not care whether the horse was still under him on the far side, or not. He instead remained upon the wide trail up through two steep canyons as far as a surprisingly handsome and well-grassed big plateau, which he did not cross, but which he rode out and around, keeping to the covert as much as possible, to still another upland flat, and there he encountered his first difficulty.

There were three log cabins on the far side of this second well-watered, secluded place, with smoke rising thinly straight up into the cold early-morning air from all three stone chimneys. He paused, made a thoughtful study of those distant residences, then shook his head and told the bay horse that if those were Indians living over there, he'd eat his hat, then they pressed along, went through a high gunsight-like slot, and saw below them a vastness which had not changed in a thousand years, and which had not changed in its most substantial aspects in probably ten thousand years.

He also saw the distant cubes cast at random in a cluster upon the vast plain which marked the location of a town. It lay southwesterly, and although he had tended in that same direction for many hours, he had still not gone far enough southward. Not that it mattered.

He wondered about a name like Las Cruces, but he'd heard long ago that in the Southwest, originally colonised and settled by the Spanish and, more recently, the Mexicans, that most towns had names like that, which did not have any meaning whatsoever to someone like Clay Anderson who knew no Spanish. Some of the damned names were real tongue-twisters, too. He had no difficulty pronouncing Las Cruces, primarily because he'd heard it spoken and had never had to try and create his own pronunciation from having seen it written, first, but he'd seen some of those oldtime names that were as long as a man's arm, and pretty darned frustrating to say.

He stopped where sunshine reached into a little grassy place, hobbled the bay, slipped off the bridle, loosened the cinch, and let the horse wander out where a thin little shallow stream of cold water crossed through a miniature jungle of grass and weeds. He strolled back to an ancient, punky old deadfall pine, sat upon it to roll a smoke for breakfast, and revelled in the wonderful newday warmth upon his head and shoulders. The cigarette was a poor substitute for a real breakfast, but on the other hand it was better than sitting there sucking air.

He had seen no sign, but then it had been either dark or not very light, ever since he'd left the shack at Carleton's Meadow, and now, upon the heights where he had a good view in most directions, he felt no apprehension. In fact, he smiled to himself about Jack Barron's probable reaction to that skimpy note he'd left, down there, and watched his backtrail, as much of it as he could see, wondering how long it would take Jack to come storming up into the mountains.

He did not feel especially hungry, particularly after the cigarette. He stubbed it out, pitched it into the weeds, and twisted comfortably to catch as much of the warm sunlight as he could. There were still some bunched-up muscles which hadn't been able to loosen away from the chill. As he turned, he raked a casual glance round-about—and saw the two dark man-shapes standing motionless watching him at a distance of about a hundred yards, both of them in the lee of a forest giant. All the hair at the nape of his neck stood up.

The two men were more shadow than substance, yet there was no mistaking either of them. They both had Winchesters hooked across their arms, and they were rather lean, lanky individuals.

He sat as still as stone for a long time, then told himself it was useless to try for the gun in his hip-holster, so he did the best he could, he raised his right hand palm forward and casually called over. "You fellers wouldn't happen to have any coffee, would you?"

Both the man-shaped shadows remained like carvings for almost a full minute, then the lead one stepped out soundlessly, crossed from forest gloom to sunshine, and Clay had his first good look at them. They were 'breeds; dark-skinned, black-haired, stalwart men, younger than

Clay and dressed in a hodge-podge which included red-skin moccasins, whiteskin britches and woollen shirts, with beaded sheaths for their large belt-knives. Neither of them carried a Colt, but they both had shell-belts looped loosely round their middles full of Winchester slugs.

When they reached the far end of the old deadfall one of them leaned his carbine upon the old tree and studied Clay stonily before speaking. His companion, a couple of paces behind, seemed less interested in Clay than he was in the saddled bay horse, unmindfully grazing a hundred yards away.

"Where you goin'?" asked the foremost of the 'breeds. "That your horse out yonder?"

Clay answered, and at the same time kept his right hand well clear of the gun on his hip. "Goin' down to that town, yonder. Las Cruces. And yes, that's my horse yonder. You fellers live up in here?"

The 'breed nodded. "Yeah. And we don't like strangers in our country."

Clay smiled. "Don't worry about that. As soon as I bridle up, I'll be gone out of here for good."

The second 'breed, who, upon closer inspection, turned out to be younger than the hard-faced 'breed, turned and put his black gaze upon Clay, then ignored him to address his companion.

"Mighty nice horse," he said.

Clay breathed in deeply, and let it all out very slowly.

It'd be a hell of a thing, getting killed up in a place like this, where nobody'd ever find a man, but if they thought they were going to acquire the bay horse, they were sure as hell going to have to earn him, and the only way they could do that would be to salt down his owner.

The foremost 'breed did not take his eyes off Clay. "Did you come from down in Tiburon?" he asked.

Clay had only heard that name once or twice before, but he didn't have to be told it was the town Mosely and his possemen had ridden out from, so he shook his head. "Nope. I really come from Montana, far up north. Then I got lost in the fog." Clay shrugged, feeling no need to say more. "I've never even seen Tiburon."

The 'breed sighed, looked indifferently out where the bay was grazing, then swung his head back and said, "Go on. Get your horse and ride down out of here."

His companion stiffened. "Let him go on foot."

Without even turning, the older hunter said it again. "Get on your bay horse and get out of these mountains." Then he turned on his companion. "You got nine good horses." He glared, and Clay got the impression that the eldest 'breed was a man people did not dispute with if they could avoid doing so. The younger 'breed sulked, and as Clay slid off the deadfall to go forth and fetch back his horse, the younger man glared venomously at him.

"I'll fight you for the horse," he said.

Clay sized up the sinewy, lanky youth, then faced the

older man, wagging his head. "You better talk him out of that notion, Mister."

The older man's low, broad brow acquired two deep lines across it. It was not an angry look, it was rather a quizzical scowl of doubt. "He don't mean with guns, cowboy," stated the older man.

Clay hadn't thought the challenge had meant weapons. "All the same, better talk him out of it, Mister."

The older hunter straightened up off the deadfall. Evidently his generosity hadn't been very strongly motivated because he motioned, now, with his Winchester barrel. "Put the gun on the log," he ordered, and before Clay could comply, he also said, "Go ahead," to the younger 'breed.

Clay stood watching. When the younger 'breed leaned his carbine and started round the butt of the old deadfall, Clay sized him up again, then slid a quick look at the pointed barrel of the other 'breed's Winchester. He slowly lifted out the Colt, resignedly placed it atop the punky bog old log, placed his shapeless hat there, too, and snugged up his roper's gloves as he stepped sidewards away from the log.

When the younger man paused, crouched slightly, then came on again in a stealthy, crab-like manner, Clay said, watching the younger 'breed closely but addressing the older man, "I don't want to do this, Mister. It's not my idea."

The older hunter did not respond with so much as a

flicker of understanding, although he surely understood. He simply kept Clay covered with his weapon, and stood there watching.

Overhead, some raucous blue-jays in the high treetops began their insistent scolding. Otherwise, there was not a sound as Clay stood relaxed and waiting.

SEVEN
"REL-YEN-OS"

CLAY HAD no qualms, but when the oncoming younger man sidled slightly so as to come in from Clay's left, that beaded scabbard showed and Clay changed his attitude a little. The man with the Winchester had made Clay disarm himself, but he'd neglected to do this for his friend, and a knife as large, and undoubtedly as sharp as this hunter's knife would be, in a close fight, could make all the difference.

Clay moved, finally, changing his tactics and not willing, now, for the younger man to hold the initiative. He turned lightly to his left, facing the younger man, then he swiftly advanced two paces to feint the younger man into an attack. But the 'breed stepped away, instead, and started that circling round to Clay's opposite side again.

One thing was obvious; this young buck might be a 'breed Indian, but he did not fight like one. Indians were courageous enough, they just were never very practical in-fighters, they had their stylised ritualistic ways of hand-battling. It never matched the completely pragmatic and absolutely functional way that white men did their in-fighting.

This young man, also, was not completely inexperienced. Maybe Clay should have suspected as much when the buck had challenged him so quickly, but at least he now faced the younger man with more respect, and prudence. When the 'breed kept sidling to the right, Clay turned again, to face him, and this time he tried stepping away to draw the buck in.

That also failed. Clay dropped his arms and gazed at the youth. He'd made another damned mistake in thinking he could put this man down fast. He stood there allowing the Indian to size him up as he minced forward, balancing forward, then Clay raised his thick arms again, and decided to allow the buck first strike. The 'breed, though, did not come straight in, he started to, then reversed himself and sprang sidewards, ducked low and came in very fast. He had an edge in youth, and in agility. He was slightly taller than Clay, but he was also about thirty pounds lighter, with the speed of a snake.

He struck, coming in below Clay's guard. The blow connected but did no damage and Clay chopped downwards—missing by a foot.

The younger man pulled back, straightened up and grinned. Clay grinned back, not because he felt like grinning, though, and now he started stalking the 'breed.

He could get no closer than the younger man allowed him to get, so he finally straightened up, turned his back, went over to the deadfall and leaned there, facing his adversary.

The younger man straightened, stared, then, with a frown beginning to show, he walked ahead. That was his first mistake. Clay's bootheel was solidly planted. When the youth was less than fifteen feet distant, Clay snapped his leg straight, catapulted ahead too fast for the younger man to jump clear, and sank his right fist to the wrist into the youth's middle.

The buck gasped and involuntarily doubled down. Clay could have clubbed him to his knees, instead, he reached, got a fistful of cloth, hauled the youth upright by sheer strength, and flung him backwards. The 'breed landed hard on his back, and with a cry of fury rolled over, came up onto his knees and whirled, knife in hand.

Clay looked swiftly to his right. The older hunter was still holding his Winchester up and aimed. He said nothing, and his face showed nothing. He obviously was not going to say anything about the knife.

Clay pulled down a big breath, let it out slowly and started forward. He was still exercising prudence, but now he was angry. More indignant, actually, than angry, but under these circumstances there was practically no difference as he stalked the younger man.

That blow in the midriff had hurt the younger man. He

showed it in his expression as he started circling again, this time holding his knife low and sidewards for a dead-ahead plunge. Only novices ever struck downwards, overhand, in a knife attack, and this youth was no novice.

But neither was Clay Anderson. He kept pressing the young 'breed, kept trying to close with him, forcing him to shift his stance and change his position from moment to moment, and when he thought it would work, he straightened up as though to pause, drawing the 'breed into a stationary stance. Then he kicked out as hard as he could, caught the low-held fist and knife in the deep gullet between his bootheel and sole, and followed this up with a two-handed attack.

The buck's knife sailed mid-way to the old deadfall and lay in the sunbright grass. The man himself, shocked and in pain, tried to dive for the knife, which was much too far.

Clay caught him fifty feet short of the knife, whirled him by his woollen shirt, and struck him twice, once with his left hand, then much harder with his knotty right fist. The young man fell in a limp heap.

Clay stepped over, picked up the knife, turned and hurled it into the forest as far as he could. Then he faced the buck with the Winchester, waiting for whatever happened next.

The older hunter lowered his weapon and leaned again upon the deadfall, gazing at Clay. "You had the right to stick him," he said, quietly.

Clay was angry and breathing hard. "I didn't want to stick him, damn it. All I wanted was to ride on out of here."

The older man said, "Do it. Get on your horse and ride out."

Clay picked his hat and pistol off the log, dropped one into its holster, crushed the other one upon his head, and walked angrily out where the bay horse, full now as a tick, was drowsing in the hot sunlight. He yanked loose the hobbles, slid in the bit and set the buckles, then tugged up the cincha and stepped up over leather. He reined back in the direction of the deadfall because that was where the trail lay, and as he came close the older hunter, still ignoring his unconscious friend in the grass, said, "Maybe, if you wanted to stay, the others wouldn't care."

"Stay," exclaimed Clay. "Stay up here? Mister, if you gave me all these damned mountains from one end to the other, I'd give 'em right back." He looked down at the still form in the grass. "I think he's got a busted wrist. I'm sorry about that."

The older man spared a casual glance for his fallen companion. "It's a lesson. He was due to learn one." The black eyes lifted. "You ever hear of Jack Barron, back down there?"

Clay leaned on the saddlehorn, beginning to breathe a little easier. "Yeah, I've heard of him. In fact, we was together only yesterday."

The buck's eyes widened slightly. "Why didn't you tell us that?"

"What the hell difference would that make?"

"Plenty difference. He's our friend. We wouldn't have made you fight."

Clay considered the stalwart hunter, then, without saying another word, he shook his head in monumental disgust, lifted his rein-hand and rode on over to the trail, heading across about a half mile of more or less level country before it dipped downward, upon the far side of the mountains, overlooking all that vast expanse of plain far below, which was now just beginning to acquire a slight, but definite, heat-haze.

Two hours later, he came upon a blue-water pool where a stream had got dammed up by deadfalls and huge boulders. He tied the horse in some trees, stripped down and waded into the water, which was nowhere nearly as cold as he had thought it would be. He bathed, and swam, and loafed upon the grassy bank until the sun had dried him, then got dressed and rode onward again. That swim made all the difference in the world in his outlook, but he was still disgusted with himself. Nothing he had done so far had been very intelligent. At least it certainly seemed that way to him.

By the time he ultimately reached the lower foothills where there was more graze and fewer trees, the sun was on its downward course. He studied it, in relation to that distant town, but in order to accomplish this he had to lift the bay horse over into a mile-consuming lope and hold him to it for the better part of an hour, then 'blow' him for another hour before boosting him over into the same loping gait again.

He saw bands of half-wild cattle, all branded. He also started up a big bunch of horses, and they acted a lot more than just half-wild as they flung up their heads, raised their tails like scorpions at sight of a rider, and left a reddish plume of dust hanging in the late-day sunlight as they raced away, following out the circling big bend of a mountain-slope.

When he was close enough, even though the sun was gone now, he could still make out the buildings of Las Cruces. Some of them, the newer ones, evidently, were made of logs from the distant mountains, but mostly, the town was adobe; adobe blocks in the walls of the houses, in the walls around the ancient plaza, and even in some of the horse corrals which lay behind the central business area.

He forgot about the 'breeds. He almost forgot about his scheme to entice Jack Barron over here after him. He had never before seen a genuine Southwestern adobe town before. In the more northerly areas of New Mexico where there was abundant timber—and also fewer native Mexicans—towns, like ranch buildings, were all of wood.

He was close enough to catch some of the smells, too,

by the time dusk was pacing inward, just ahead of him, and they made him remember that he had been a long while without a meal.

He entered Las Cruces from the northeast, rode between rows of *jacals* in Mex-town, passed a very old plaza with the customary big well in the centre of it, surrounded by a walkway and a waist-high adobe wall, looked with frank interest at several ornately attired bronzed horsemen he passed, riding saddles with no swells and enormous saddlehorns, then he passed through into the main thoroughfare, saw the liverybarn sign, and turned towards it. Leaving Mex-town and passing over into *gringo*-town, was like going out of one completely alien world into another world which was totally different, but, to Clay Anderson, familiar in just about all its aspects.

He stepped down between the carriage lamps on the front of the liverybarn, and whistled up a hostler, a grey-haired, mahogany older Mex with a smile that fairly dazzled Clay, because squarely in the front of it the old man had four magnificent, highly polished gold teeth.

He flipped a silver coin to the hostler, left explicit instructions on how he wanted his horse cared for, then he patted the bay's powerful rump as he was led away, turned and sniffed.

It was supper time in *gringo*-town. In Mex-town people very often ate quite late at night, because, this time of year, when it was seasonally hot, autumn or not, the dark-hided natives had a habit of sleeping away most of the afternoon, a custom which left them wide awake long after the more prosaic *gringos,* who rarely napped in the daytime, had eaten and were yawning.

He took a chance and entered a Mexican restaurant. He had eaten chili and beans many times, but when the meal was finally set before him in Las Cruces, the chili-beans were only on the side. The main course were four elongated, flat-looking things that when he scraped one with his fork, showed a bizarre, cooked green colour beneath. He tried it, with strong doubts. It had a flavour like nothing he had ever tasted before. It was, in fact, delicious. He ate all four of those critters, then drank thick coffee, and when the perspiring fat proprietor came along to re-fill the coffee cup, Clay said, "What were those things you fed me, Mister?" The Mexican looked steadily at Clay for a moment, and he smiled broadly.

"Newcomer," he announced, in a musical accent.

Clay nodded. "It's an odd name for 'em, but they were mighty tasty."

"No, *Señor,*" said the Mexican, fighting back laughter. "*You* are the newcomer." He poked his finger into the empty plate. "What you ate—those were *relleños.*"

"What?"

The Mexican put down the coffee pot, leaned down and contorted his very dark face in all seriousness. "*Señor*, say after me: Rel."

"Rel."

"Yen—os."

"Yen—os." Clay formed his mouth to put it all into an undivided sequence. "*Relleños*." He grinned. "Do you know how to spell it?"

"No, *Señor*. I only know how to speak it."

Clay arose, shook the Mexican's hand, handed over the price of his meal and walked out of the little cafe a bilingual man—he knew one Spanish word.

All he had to do now was locate someone named Cantrell.

EIGHT

LAS CRUCES

IN THE oldtime Southwestern cowtown segregation was a viable factor; many of the big cow outfits had *vaqueros* and cowboys working together and sharing the bunkhouses, while in towns like Las Cruces there were distinctly two separate enclaves, the *gringo* and the beaner sections. But if segregation had, in part, its foundations in the ethnic difference, that was not really why the races lived apart yet mingled more or less freely. It was language, custom, tradition, but mostly it was language. The cowmen who took over the Southwest could learn new customs, and in fact they did, every one of them, and most of them also adopted Mex values, but in every saloon—or *cantina*—every blessed night of the week for all the bilinguals in there, there were five times as many who could speak one language but not the other. Usually, though, native *gringo* stockmen were as fluent in Spanish as in English—and wonderfully ungrammatical in both.

Clay got a sample of this bizarre cosmopolitanism in the first saloon he entered after eating the flat, green, stuffed pepper. The place was like every other saloon west of the Missouri in two respects—it was predominately patronised by rangemen, and it was full of smoke—but it was also different in that all along the bar, and among the scattered tables, men were speaking three languages: English, Spanish, and a kind of English-Spanish combination that was harder by far to learn, than either of the other two languages.

He got a place at the bar, waited patiently for the barman to come along and bring him a glass of rye whiskey, then he turned and looked out over the room. He had never seen anything quite like it before. *Vaqueros* did not dress like cowboys, for one thing, and most of the *gringo* cowboys in the room did not dress like *vaqueros,* but they had far too much silver on them to mix well, back in Montana. Clay rather liked it. He liked seeing handsomely inlaid and engraved spur-shanks, intricately filigreed silver buckles, and even the few heavily blued sixguns around the room which had been very painstakingly silver inlaid in very handsome designs. In fact, when one blue-eyed big cowboy walked past, close to Clay, it was Clay's opinion that maybe up in Montana someone would kill him just to own his gun, it was so fancy.

Another man might have indulgently smiled. Clay didn't because he knew tophands when he saw them. This saloon was full of them. He turned back, facing across the bar gazing at a powerfully muscled-up black bull with white horns dropping his head on a twisting run to gore the white-faced matador upon the ground. It was laid out terribly vividly in a really magnificent painting over the backbar. In Montana, by now drunken cowboys would have shot that painted bull full of holes, and would have sneered at the man on the ground, who went to face the bull without wearing his Colt.

Clay was a man of perception. He understood the difference between his world and this world. He did not necessarily approve of much that he saw, now, but it was certainly interesting. Beside him on the right, a *gringo* and a *vaquero* were speaking back and forth in that half-halfty border lingo, and doing it as though they'd been born speaking nothing else. On his left two older cowmen, grey and grizzled, both *gringos,* were discussing rangeland conditions. They, at least, sounded no different from their counterparts in the high north country. Then one of them said, "I'm not going to push south for clean-up feed this year, I think I'll go onto the old Cantrell range."

The other cowman stiffly pointed to their emptied

glasses when the barman came along, then picked up his end of the conversation while eyeing the bottle in the barman's hand. "Unless the old lady's come down a hell of a lot, it won't pay. She's been a thorn in my side for years, adjoinin' me, and never letting anyone, but especially me, her neighbour, use up her dry feed the end of the season. If you pay her price, Sam, you might as well give her every fourth or fifth fat calf you got."

Sam picked up his re-filled glass, balancing it perfectly in a stone-steady hand. "I know. I know how she is as well as you do, but I'm going to try something different. I'm going to drift the smallest herd up there first; just drift 'em mind you, and then go back for the big herd. There won't be no shod-horsetracks, and the law says if you don't want cattle on your land, you got to fence 'em *out,* their owner don't have to fence 'em *in.*"

"It won't work," stated the other cowman. "Len'll turn 'em back."

Sam laughed, downed his whiskey and turned to drop a sly look upon his friend. "Maybe the little band, Hank, but don't no solitary rider, good or not, turn back three thousand cattle, and keep 'em turned back." Sam put aside his emptied glass, leaned down and softly said, "Then, after I've had the clean-up feed, I'll ride up there and pay the old woman exactly what it's worth. Next year, by gawd, she'll have seen the light."

Clay finished his rye liquor, rolled a smoke, pondered the fairness of Sam's tough idea, shrugged it off as none of his blessed business, and sauntered back out into the magnificent star-washed black velvet desert night.

There were very few people abroad in *gringo*-town, but over in Mex-town there were strollers, even a few sad-songed guitarists, along with some old men who ritually sat almost every warm night upon the broad, low steps of the little mud church, to talk beyond the harassment of grandchildren.

Clay strolled the town, then headed for the liverybarn to look in on his horse, but that was not the only reason. What a man did not learn in a cowtown saloon, he could surely learn at the liverybarn.

The nighthawk was that same gold-fanged, ageing Mexican the colour of polished latigo Clay had handed his horse over to earlier. The hostler was seated out front along the white-washed mud wall of the old building, smoking a brown-paper cigarette when Clay sauntered up and sank down beside him, saying, "Good evening, partner."

The Mexican smiled, showing his splendid gold teeth. *"Buenas noches, amigo; que paso?"*

Clay sighed, fished around for his makings and hunched down as he rolled the cigarette. "Mister," he said, with solemn patience. "I don't speak Spanish. In fact, until a couple of hours ago, I didn't know one single word of Spanish. Right now, all I can say in Spanish is *relleño*."

The grizzled Mexican turned, looked long at Clay,

then doubled over in mirth.

Clay lit up, eyed the hostler patiently, and even smiled a little when the hostler finally straightened up squeezing tears from the outer edges of his eyes with a soiled shirtsleeve. Then the Mexican tapped Clay's arm and said, "*Pardona mi, compadre*. I don't mean to laugh on you. But—*relleño*—well, you see, *compadre, Norte-americanos* don't learn a word like *relleño* first, they learn *bastardo, hijo mano*—something like 'go hit your mother'."

Clay inhaled, exhaled, studied his companion then said, "Go hit your mother?"

"*Si, vaquero*. Yes, cowboy. In Spanish it is very bad thing to say to someone."

Clay considered the growing ash on his smoke. "Go hit your mother," he muttered, and gently shook his head. "If you say so, Mister." He eyed the Mexican again. "Tell me something; do you know anyone named Cantrell in these parts?"

"Oh yes, *amigo*. It is an old family—for *gringos*."

"And where, exactly, do they live—*amigo?*"

The Mexican gestured expansively. "Up the stageroad about six or seven miles, *Señor*. There is an old tree and beside this old tree, the ruts go west to the buildings."

Clay accepted that. He would be able to find the place. Now, he moved on to what came next. "They own a lot of land hereabouts, do they?"

The Mexican shrugged. "*Señor*, when I was a young

man I saw the man get hanged. Right here in this town. He was a *pistolero,* but they hanged him for also being a rider of other people's horses, as I recall. But yes, he claimed miles of the range country north and west of Las Cruces. His family still holds it. But what you asked—do they *own* the land—I can tell you, *amigo,* that to own land in this territory is simply to be able to take it and hold it. *Señor* Cantrell was *mala hombre*—a very bad man. What good is the land to you, *amigo,* if you get killed trying to keep it against such a man as *Señor* Cantrell."

Clay sighed. There was nothing exactly novel about cowmen claiming land and holding it, but generally this was only done with unclaimed land. There was one breed of men, though, who came too late for the free land, so they did it the other way, the way this beaner was talking about, they arrived out of nowhere with big bands of cattle, a few illiterate, troublesome riders—usually Texans—squatted on someone's land, and if the former grazer could not, or would not, chouse them away, they took the land and held it—with their weapons. They were the free-graze men. They were also distrusted, scorned, and ostracised by other cattlemen. They were pariahs.

The Mexican beside Clay put out his brown-paper cigarette, glanced at the clear, clean-sweep of high heaven, then re-settled himself upon the wall-bench as he said, "*Amigo,* if you are going out there to get work, I can tell you—it would be much better if you went almost any-where else."

Clay could have agreed with that, and he'd never yet even seen a Cantrell. He changed the topic by asking about law enforcement in Las Cruces. The Mexican shrugged. "We have the sheriff. His name is Burt Meredith. He is a good man." The hostler shrugged elo-quently. "But this is a very large land, *Señor*."

Clay was able to corroborate that; he'd seen the extent of this southwesterly country from a mountaintop, and it was indeed large. "You mean Sheriff Meredith don't always catch the law-breakers, *amigo?*" he asked.

The Mexican turned a kindly, dark face. "Very seldom, *Señor,* does he catch the law-breakers. This is not only a big country, *amigo,* but the Mexican border is not so ter-ribly far. If a man commits a crime in the night, when it's almost impossible to track him, by morning if he owns a good horse, he can be almost down to the border. When the sheriff leaves town, you must understand, the next morning . . ." The hostler's shoulders rose, and fell. "Even killing a good horse isn't enough. You under-stand?"

Clay understood. For a while he sat comfortably silent watching horsemen moving back and forth in the north-ward roadway, up where the saloon was, and where the cafes were still lighted and doing business. He fished in a pocket, pulled forth some squashed-flat, sweat-curled bank notes which looked as though he had been carrying them for months on end—which he had—peeled off a fair-sized one and offered it to the Mexican as he said, "What's your name, Mister?"

The hostler looked from the proffered greenback to Clay's face, without making any attempt to accept the money. "Gutierrez, *Señor*."

Clay sighed. "I couldn't never roll them r's right. You don't happen to have another name?"

"Eusebio, *Señor*. That is my name. Eusebio Gutierrez."

Clay considered, then said, "Well sir, suppose I just call you Pete."

Eusebio Gutierrez very slightly inclined his head, still gazing steadily into Clay's face and still making no move to take the greenback. "All right, *Señor*. What do I call you?"

"Clay. That's easy enough, isn't it?"

"Yes. Clay. All right, Clay. What is the money for— your horse's care?"

"Nope. There is a young feller going to ride into Las Cruces maybe in the morning, maybe tomorrow afternoon. I want you to tell me how you'll be able to let me know when he arrives, if I'm a few miles up-country beyond town."

Gutierrez still made no move to touch the money. "Clay—is this man a *pistolero*, or maybe a lawman?"

"Well, he's sure as hell no lawman, Pete," replied Clay, and shoved the greenback into Gutierrez's hand.

"I'll give you his description, and when he rides in— how can you signal to me that he's arrived?"

Eusebio Gutierrez considered the greenback. It was a lot of money to him. "When I was a boy, *Señor* Clay, and the Indians came riding around here, my father and the other men would build a nice fire on the outskirts of town to warn all the outlying *rancheros,* and also to signal the army camp which used to be over against the foothills."

Clay nodded. "Sure. With smoke-signals."

"No," stated Gutierrez. "Smoke signals can't be seen very far on a sunny day, *Señor*. My father and the other men would wait until the fire was burning very well, then they would throw greens on it, to make smoke, and they would then throw on some red oxide, and the smoke would turn the colour of blood. You could see such smoke for a hundred miles." Eusebio Gutierrez, seeing the admiring look on Clay's face, smiled, pocketed the greenback, and asked a question.

"How will I know this man?"

Clay went to work describing not only Jack Barron, but also his black horse.

NINE

LEN CANTRELL

ON THIS side of the mountains, far from Carleton's Meadow, the mornings were much warmer than they had been over in the fog-bank country.

They were also clear as glass when Clay mounted up out front of the liverybarn, winked at Eusebio Gutierrez, his new friend, and rode away. For Gutierrez, earning the money Clay had given him was not a problem; he would be glad to signal the arrival in Las Cruces of this other *gringo*. What bothered him was that, although Clay had said the other *gringo* was not a lawman, he had neglected also to say he was not a *pistolero,* and any sane man would prefer crossing a lawman to crossing a gunfighter.

Still it was a lot of money. And if Clay never mentioned their arrangement, Eusebio Gutierrez certainly would never mention it, therefore the matter should end there.

He had had all night to make his judgement of Clay. When he stood out front in the very early dawnlight watching Clay ride northward out of town, he was entirely satisfied about the *gringo vaquero;* he was not a man to make trouble for a friend. Gutierrez shrugged. But he was obviously a man who could indeed make trouble for someone he did not like.

The sun was slow rising. Clay was three miles north of Las Cruces before it appeared above a far-curving, uneven horizon. By the time it had cleared those faraway humps, he had loped another mile and a half, and in that glass-clear air, he saw the distant tree at the side of the stageroad.

He cut inland more than a mile south of the tree, angling northwesterly. He had no actual plan, just a forthright idea. He was seeking a face-down between Jack Barron and Len Cantrell, with himself between them. Maybe it wasn't a very sly idea, but then Clay Anderson was not a very sly individual.

He could distantly see the old tree as he rode parallel to it, westerly, but although he looked in every direction he saw no ranch buildings, and the Mex hostler had said the Cantrell place was only a few miles inland, so he should be able to see the buildings soon.

Eventually, he saw a few old cows with fine, fat calves by their sides, but in all the small bands he passed, the total number of animals did not exceed one hundred head, counting calves, which was a very insignificant herd to be running over all the grassland he could also see, in every direction.

There were no fences, but that would be natural; even the children of an old free-grazer would be prejudiced against fencing. Clay wasn't a free-grazer and never had been one, but he was also prejudiced against barbed wire.

He rode over a low, broad roll of range and in the fold of ground on the far side he started up a little bank of marked horses. They probably wouldn't have fled so precipitously if he hadn't come onto them so abruptly, but by the time they saw him, he was less than about two hundred yards away, and that was enough to spook almost any range animal.

The brand was a Walking C on the left shoulder. He saw that much before the horses became a blur of speed heading eastward. He stopped in the little warm swale where they had been grazing to roll a smoke, lit up, snapped the match, picked up his reins and twisted in the saddle to glance around.

There was a solitary horseman coming towards him in a fast run off about half a mile. He turned the bay facing in this new direction, folded both hands calmly atop the saddlehorn and waited as he watched.

The rider was lean and long-legged, wore a battered, dusty old brown hat, a blue, rumpled workshirt that hung like sacking, and, Mex style, carried a rawhide quirt on the right wrist, along with the spurs on each heel which cowboys usually figured was all they needed, unless of course they were Southwesterners, then they also carried those rawhide whips.

Clay lifted his hand in an easy salute as the oncoming rider slackened speed a little, then waited for the salute to be returned. It was, eventually, but not very enthusiastically, Clay sighed; this was the darnedest country for folks being on the peck all the time he'd ever been in. He eased his right hand back and tugged loose the tie-down on his hip-holstered Colt, then he methodically peeled off his gloves and stuffed them under his belt.

The rider came up another hundred feet or so, hauled down to a fast walk, and finished approaching at that gait. The horse had one of those Walking C marks on his shoulder. It was a well-bred, iron-grey animal, young and durable.

The rider was a woman.

Clay blew smoke when he realised this, thumbed back his hat and made a smile as he threw forth a greeting. "Morning, Ma'am. Sure is a fine day."

She stopped thirty feet off, studied Clay for a moment, then said, "Why did you spook those horses?"

Clay was taken entirely by surprise. He looked over his shoulder, but the horses were no longer anywhere in sight, so he turned back facing her. "I didn't spook them. Well; if I did, I sure didn't mean to. I had no idea you was after them. I just rode over that swell back yonder, and . . ."

"Who are you?" the woman demanded.

"Name is Clay Anderson."

"Didn't you see the warning burned into the tree alongside the road?"

Clay was slow replying. She was in her twenties and pretty as a speckled pony, with coppery-coloured dark hair, skin the shade of new-minted gold, and was hung together the way the Good Lord knew a female had ought to be hung together. And ornery, obviously. Everyone in New Mexico Territory was ornery.

"Ma'am, I didn't come by the tree, I cut inland back a few miles. What kind of a warning is burnt into the tree?"

"Keep out. That's the warning."

"Well, Ma'am, I sort of have business with some folks who live hereabouts, and I thought I'd just ride in and speak my piece and . . ."

"What folks have you business with?" she barked.

"The Cantrells, Ma'am."

The beautiful eyes flickered a little, looked up and down, looked at the loose gun in Clay's holster, at his powerful bay horse, then she said, "What business, Mister?"

He was tiring of this, so he leaned slightly on the saddlehorn when he said, "That'll be between me and the Cantrells, I expect. Particularly, I'm looking for a feller by the name of Len Cantrell."

The girl's annoyance vanished, her eyes widened slowly, then she said, "You're a stranger aren't you?"

Clay did not deny that. "Green as grass in this part of the country."

"You'd have to be, Mister, to be looking for a feller named Len Cantrell."

Clay stared. "He's dead, then?"

"Mister, he's not a *feller*. I'm Lenore Cantrell. Folks

have called me Len since I was three or four years old."

Clay continued to lean and look steadily across the little intervening distance. The shock was bad enough, but the surprise, and its confusing implications, was worse. He cleared his throat, reached up to push back his hat, looked away, then looked back at her. "You're not joshing with me, are you?"

"Why? I don't know you."

He nodded sceptically. "I should have figured something like this would happen. I should have known. I'll tell you frankly, Ma'am, this is the—darnedest—country I was ever in." He did not take his eyes off her. "You don't by any chance have a brother?"

"There is only my mother and me. My father's been dead since I was a baby, just about. No, I have no brother. I have no kin at all, except my mother." Lenore Cantrell paused and faintly frowned at Clay. "Didn't anyone tell you I was a girl?"

"No Ma'am, they sure as hel—heck—didn't. And last night I talked to a Messican hostler at the liverybarn in Las Cruces."

The handsome girl said, "Eusebio Gutierrez." She said it with all the correct inflections. No one had to tell Clay this handsome woman spoke Spanish like a native. Then, loosening slightly in the saddle and considering Clay in a different mood, she almost smiled. "Well; I'm sorry to have to be such a disappointment to you, Mister Anderson, but what was it you wanted to tell Len Cantrell?"

He had no intention of telling her anything. Not yet anyway. "Where's the ranch?" he asked, and when she offered one of those expansive gestures like Gutierrez had given him last night, and which seemed to be natural with people who lived in a country this vast and sparsely settled, he straightened up with his rein-hand rising. "Let's ride on over there," he said to her, "and I'll only have to say it once. If your maw's at home."

The girl turned her iron-grey gelding to ride alongside Clay; she looked puzzled, but not the least bit apprehensive. For a half mile they rode stoically silent, then he turned, looked her over again, gently wagged his head and without speaking rode the balance of that same mile before offering to speak again.

"Tell me something, Miss Cantrell. Have you ever heard of a man named Jack Barron?"

Her tan-tawny eyes came around, drawn out narrow. "Everyone in the Territory has heard of Jack Barron. You're not going to try and tell me you are Jack Barron, are you?"

Clay did not answer her question. He asked one of his own. "Would you know him if you was to see him?"

She looked down at the plaited rawhide reins and romal in her hands and delayed her answer just a little. "If you happen to be a lawman," she eventually said, "you're wasting your time coming out here, Mister Anderson."

"Ma'am, I'm no lawman. But I'll tell you what I *am.*

A damned fool—if you'll excuse the profanity. Now then, let's try it again: Would you recognise Jack Barron if you saw him?"

She was still elusive. "Why? What difference does that make—if you're not a lawman?" Before he could answer, she flung up her head and stared at him. "A gunfighter looking for him? I don't believe it; you're too old to be a gunfighter."

Clay looped his reins, allowing the bay to plod along, fished forth his dwindling sack of tobacco, bleakly rolled a smoke he felt no need for at all, lit it, stared bitterly ahead where some trees around a stand of adobe buildings showed, then stuffed the makings back into a shirt pocket and did not speak for a hundred yards. All the time, the girl was studying him closely, but indirectly.

She prodded him. "Are you?"

She meant was he a gunfighter, but he chose acidly to interpret the question differently. "Yes, I'm too old to be a gunman."

"That's not what I meant. I meant are you . . ."

"Lady, if the folks in this country was to select someone to negotiate treaties for them, or maybe to gain the goodwill of rangemen, you'd be the last one they'd pick." Having got that off his chest, Clay turned and gave her a rough look. "No, I'm not looking for Jack Barron to gun him down. In fact, I'm not looking for the damned idiot at all. For a while yet, anyway."

They rode the balance of the distance in cold silence.

He let her lead the way across the dusty yard to the low, broad adobe barn, and when he stepped off over there in front of a log tie-rack, to loop his reins, the girl led her horse on inside the barn where he could see her proceeding with the off-saddling and un-bridling. He finished his smoke while he waited. He also turned and made a methodical study of the buildings, including the main house which was about two hundred feet southward, standing among some huge old cottonwoods, shaded and solid and very peaceful-looking. There was a veranda which ran completely around the house, a common thing in the hot Southwest where shade created dead-air space and kept things cooler.

Otherwise, the buildings looked old and solid, and just a little as though they could use a man's hand here and there. He dropped the smoke, trampled it out, turned as the lithe, high-breasted, lovely girl walked forth, told himself that if he'd known two days earlier what he knew now, he'd have pinned Jack Barron's shoulders to a wall somewhere and wrung the truth out of him, because if the girl knew *him,* it was a surefire bet he knew *her,* and yet he'd let on that she was a man, when any damned fool with just one-tenth his eyesight couldn't possibly make a mistake like that.

She returned his look, then jerked her head. "Come along to the house."

He fell in beside her, dutifully plodded along, not at all sure what he should say, now that he was here.

TEN

SOME EXPLANATIONS

THE MOTHER of Lenore Cantrell gave Clay a clue as to where her daughter had inherited the lithe, active look. She was a greying edition of her daughter, but in fact did not look to Clay, who admittedly was not the best judge, to be old enough to have a grown daughter.

He had expected something different. He was not certain what it was he had expected, but as he met Agnes Cantrell upon the veranda of the rambling old adobe ranch-house, he thought to himself that she was just about the opposite in every way from what he had expected, except when she coldly told him she did not look kindly upon trespassers.

His response to that was simple. "Lady, I didn't trespass. All my life I've respected the property rights of others. But in this case I thought it'd be better to come see you—and anyway, I never saw the tree up close, didn't even know what was burnt into it until I met your girl out yonder."

"Stampeding the horses I was trying to round up and bring in," reported Len.

Clay had had enough. He looked stonily at the women. "I didn't stampede your damned horses, young woman. If I'd wanted to stampede 'em, believe me, you'd never even have *seen* 'em." He paused, while still glaring. "And one more thing, young lady: It wouldn't have made a darned bit of difference whether I come up or not—the way you were going about it you'd never have corralled those horses." He turned towards the very handsome, greying woman. "Miz' Cantrell, I'll tell you what brought me, then I'll be on my way."

Agnes Cantrell nodded, motioned to chairs along the front of the house in the pleasant shadows, and sat down. Her skin was a shade or two darker than the shade of her daughter's skin, and she had very dark brown eyes. She was, in fact, every bit as handsome in her way, as the younger woman was in a different way. Clay had already decided that Agnes Cantrell must have been married very young.

Now, yanking a chair round where he could more nearly face her, Clay dropped down, put his hat aside, and said, "Few days back, Ma'am, I was riding through a fog so thick you could hardly count your fingers, and run onto this old abandoned ranch. There was a young feller in the barn. He took me prisoner. His name was Jack Barron. Some possemen under a feller named Whit Mosely come up next, captured the pair of us, and when we got a chance, whilst they were taking us to some town called Tiburon, Jack and I escaped. Now Ma'am, that's how I come to be over on your porch."

The dark eyes of Agnes Cantrell lingered on Clay in doubt. "I don't understand."

Clay sighed. "Ma'am, when I was a prisoner of that outlaw, we talked some. He said his ambition was to hunt down a feller who killed his folks years back."

"That feller has been dead for a great many years," stated Agnes Cantrell, with a slight sound of weariness, or resignation, in her words. "And Jack Barron's not the only one who had felt that way. I'll never get over being surprised at how long folks carry grudges, Mister Anderson. Leo Cantrell was Lenore's father and my husband. He's been dead more than twenty years. As for Jack Barron . . ."

"I'll tell him," the younger woman said, interrupting her mother. "Mister Anderson, Jack knows I'm not a man."

Clay twisted to gaze perplexedly at the girl. "Then will someone tell me why he said he was going to come over here and get his eye for an eye?"

"Three years ago Jack and I met at a dance in Las Cruces," Lenore Cantrell explained. "I had no idea who he was. He said he'd ridden over from Tiburon and that his name was John. That was about all he said while he danced, except that he was having a good time."

"What did you tell him about yourself?" asked Clay.

Lenore smiled softly. "My first name, just like he'd told me his first name. That's all. Right then, while we were dancing, it was enough. Later, we ate together at the supper the church ladies had fixed downstairs under the fire-hall in town." Lenore paused, gazing in her mother's direction. "That was when he asked me if I knew the Cantrell family and I told him that I did, so he asked me where he could best meet Len Cantrell for a showdown, and I then, finally, asked him why he'd want that."

"And he told you," said Clay.

"Yes . . . I came home and asked my mother if it was true."

Agnes took up the story from this point on. "Mister Anderson, when my husband was riding roughshod over in the Tiburon country, I was ill in the wagon. After I had Lenore I was almost a full year regaining my strength. There was an infection, and some other complications. I did not know what my husband and those vicious, uncouth Texans who rode for him, had done. I did not know the details of all that had happened over in the Tiburon country until after he'd been hanged over in Las Cruces. Then Burt Meredith, the local lawman, rode out one day and showed me a whole bundle of depositions and other accounts he'd accumulated. I never mentioned any of this to Len. Not while she was growing up, but eventually I had to tell her—the night she came home from that dance, I finally had to let her know the full truth."

Clay leaned back. "I'm plumb sorry," he told Agnes, and meant each word of it. "When did Jack find out Len was a girl?"

"Last summer," stated Lenore. "I never forgot him,

naturally, and when some of our cows strayed into the foothills over on the east range and I went after them, there were some 'breed Indians over there getting ready to round up our strays and drive them up into the mountains. I was alone or maybe I'd have done differently, Mister Anderson."

Clay waited, beginning to have a hunch about how this lithe girl had reacted, based upon how she had reacted to his presence on Cantrell range earlier.

"I got into a spit of tree, Mister Anderson, and began firing over their heads."

Clay inclined his head gently, having expected her to say something like this. "You hit any of 'em?"

"No, I wasn't trying to hurt anyone, just to scare them off."

"Did you succeed?"

"Yes. They scattered like birds, and I rode down there swiftly, before the 'breeds got organised again, lit in behind our cows and pushed them as hard as I could for home. I made it, too, but that evening when I went down to the barn to chuck feed to the horse I'd used, just as I was forking the hay over the corral, a man stepped up, took the pitchfork from me, shoved me against the back of the barn and raised his gun. There was a moon that night. He stood there for a full couple of minutes like he'd just seen a ghost. Then he said, 'By gawd, *you!* I don't believe it'. Mister Anderson, he wasn't any more surprised than I was. It was John, the feller I'd met at the dance several years earlier. We just sort of looked at one another for a while, then he put up the gun and asked me if my name was Cantrell. I said it was, that in fact my name was Lenore, just like I'd told him at the dance, but that folks had always called me Len—and that I was the 'feller' he'd wanted to meet some years back. He— swore. When he got over that, he told me who *he* was, Jack Barron, the surviving member of that family my father had—made all that trouble for long ago. As soon as he said Barron, I knew who he was. I also knew he was an outlaw, because I'd heard a little about him in town. Not much, because he's not as well known over here as he is across the mountains. I accused him of being a cattle thief, and of riding with those 'breeds. He told me the 'breeds were the only people he trusted and that he lived up there on the mountaintops with them, some of the time." Lenore stopped speaking, glanced from Clay to her mother, then back to Clay again. "I told Jack Barron I didn't even know what my father had done until a couple of years earlier, but that if he was dead-set on fighting the Cantrells for something neither he nor I had any hand in, I'd go up to the house and get my gun, and come right back. Then I walked away."

Clay looked at Agnes, who gently smiled at him as though she, too, thought the idea of a girl fighting a man with a gun were preposterous. Clay looked back at the younger woman. "And . . . ?"

"I went back down there, behind the barn, with my gun

buckled on—and Jack Barron was gone."

Clay fished forth his tobacco sack and papers. As he did this he glanced at Agnes. "Do you mind, Ma'am?"

Her smile lingered. "Not at all, Mister Anderson."

Clay rolled the cigarette and lit it, then sat back, crossing one thick leg over the other leg as he put a faintly frowning look upon Lenore Cantrell. "Well, young lady, I'm not here to pass any judgements, but all the same I got to tell you . . . that sure wasn't any way for a lady to act."

Lenore flared out at him. "What was I supposed to do—wait for him to shoot me?"

"He wouldn't have shot you."

"Wouldn't he, then? You're that sure?"

Clay nodded. "I'm that sure. I'm older than you or him. I've spent my whole life among rangemen. I've known a few two-bit outlaws in my time, and he's no different from the others. Actually, as an outlaw, he's a pretty poor example. Anyway, that's neither here nor there since it happened and nothing came of it. But you see, what I was trying to do, Ma'am, was make him see how damned silly this idea of his, about being an outlaw, really is, so I deliberately baited him into coming over here. My reason was to be here when he showed up, and make him see how foolish it is for a grown man to pretend like he wants revenge . . . But I sure as hell never expected to find *you*. I figured on finding a *man* named Len Cantrell."

Agnes said, "Do you think he'll come, Mister Anderson?"

Clay thought so, or he wouldn't have gone to all the trouble he'd made for himself. "Yes'm. I figure he'll show up."

Lenore's steady gaze hardened towards Clay. "I'll be ready, you can bet on that."

Clay inhaled, exhaled, and kept looking at the handsome girl. "You'll do no such thing," he told her bluntly.

"He's coming after me, isn't he? Then I'll be ready."

Clay continued to gaze at the girl. He turned, finally, to look at her mother. "She's young," he said. "Maybe you and I figure this a little differently."

Agnes did not concede this, but she asked a question. "Tell me how *you* figure it, Mister Anderson."

That made him back and fill a little. What he was thinking, now that he'd seen this beautiful girl, was that no young buck including Jack Barron, the two-bit renegade, could possibly look upon Len Cantrell as a genuine enemy, and to bolster his belief, he recalled very vividly how Jack had thought, and talked constantly of the girl. He had talked of her as though she were still his enemy, as though he still thought of her as a man, but Clay was not that simple-minded. Young men did not talk about a beautiful girl, not constantly have her in their minds, unless they were very acutely conscious of the fact that she *was* a beautiful girl. The trouble was, though, he did not know how to explain this in front of the girl, to her mother, so he smoked and looked else-where, out and around the sunbright old ranchyard, and finally, when he knew he had to say *something,* he turned back towards Agnes with a careful comment.

"Why don't we just wait and see, Ma'am?"

Agnes, who had been studying Clay through his long moment of indecision, smiled. "Would you care for something to eat, Mister Anderson?" she asked, arising as though his answer had to be a foregone conclusion. She went to the door and held it open. "I was making a pot of *chili con carne* when you two rode in."

Clay, ignoring the younger woman, took a long, last pull off his cigarette, stamped it out upon the veranda flooring and arose to hitch his gunbelt into place and to also retrieve his hat.

"I'm right grateful," he said, then he looked at Lenore. "You'd best come along, too."

She looked up at Clay without speaking or without showing any expression, for a long time, but when he did not move nor look as though he might relent, she finally arose and entered the house. Clay was the last one to pass inside. He paused in the doorway for one final rearward look around, then he also went inside.

The old house was cool and shadowy, and, like most adobe ranch-houses with three-foot thick mud walls, it was soundless.

The place was furnished with heavy old Spanish chairs, tables, and horsehair sofas, all in dark wood. It was one of those Southwestern residences in the cow country that seemed to have been there for an endless length of time, and for all Clay Anderson knew at the time, it *had* been there that long.

But it was immaculate, the windows, in their deeply recessed settings, shone like crystal, and all this meant that a woman ruled here, not a man, as in most ranch-houses.

He dropped his hat upon a high-backed old carved chair and followed the women on through to the large, airy kitchen, where the aroma of simmering food, highly spiced and mouth-watering, reminded him again that, lately, he hadn't been eating very regularly nor very well.

ELEVEN
AGNES

IT WAS still early when Lenore excused herself on the grounds that there were a few more of their old cows to be brought in yet, and, with a sidelong glance at Clay, also to mention trying to locate those stampeded horses again.

He sighed and leaned to arise and go along. "You'll need help."

Lenore stared. "I've been handling these matters ever since I've been big enough to sit a horse, Mister

Anderson."

Agnes interrupted with a smile at her daughter. "Go along, Len. Just be careful. And Len . . ."

"Yes, I know, Mother. I'll stay out in the open country and keep watch." She went to the pantry door, turned, considered square-jawed burly Clay Anderson for a moment, then suddenly her entire face brightened in a smile. "I'm sorry I was so disagreeable," she said, and whisked on out of the house.

Clay looked a little helplessly from the empty pantry doorway to where Agnes was leaning to re-fill both their coffee cups. Her dark eyes swept up, showing amusement. As she finished and set the coffee pot aside, she sat back down, still looking amused.

"Mister Anderson, don't try to understand them. I can't, and a hundred years ago I was one of them; I was also her age, and with her temperament."

Clay sat comfortably in the cool, hushed old house, gazing across at the dark, flawless beauty of the greying woman. He said, "Ma'am, do you know a couple of cowmen hereabouts, one named Sam, and the other one called Hank?"

She did. "Yes indeed. One is Sam Waters, who adjoins us to the north, and I'd think the other one would be Hank Overman, who adjoins our land to the west."

"Well, Ma'am, last night in a saloon I heard them talking about running cattle on you. The feller named Sam said he'd turn in a small bunch, first, then push in about three thousand head."

The doe-like dark brown eyes brightened and hardened on Clay. "Sam is a likable man, Mister Anderson, and at times he's been a good neighbour to my daughter and me, but he's been holding back heifers for several years, and now he's got about twice as many cattle as his own range will support. He's been over here about leasing, and because I don't want him or his men riding the ranch and using our buildings, I gave him a ridiculously high figure."

Clay knew all this; at least he knew the part about the high figure. "Maybe you'd ought to talk to the lawman in Las Cruces," he said, and suddenly straightened in the chair when he heard horsemen. They had to be close by, in the yard, for him to be able to hear them at all in that fortress-like house.

He arose, as did Agnes Cantrell. She moved past him briskly and went to the parlour, then opened the door leading to the veranda. By the time Clay got out there, she was already in conversation with a man whose deep, gruff voice sounded familiar to Clay. He did not go out there at this moment, he instead crossed to a window, and leaned down to look out.

There were two lean, rangy riders still sitting their saddles out front of the house. The third saddled animal was riderless while Sam Waters argued with Agnes Cantrell upon the veranda. He was not actually arguing with her, at least he was not bullying her although he was a large, roughly-hewn man, the kind who traditionally thought in terms of roughness, but he was not allowing her to say much, and the longer he talked the more insistent he sounded, so Clay moved across to the doorway and stepped through.

All three of the men stared, but Sam Waters showed the most astonishment; his jaw sagged.

Clay used this moment well, he said, "Mister, the lady don't want to lease to you. She don't want your cattle on her range." Clay let that sink in, then he smiled a little at the older man to take some of the sting out. "Maybe next year or the year after, Mister."

Sam Waters recovered, then, and started to get red in the face. He ignored the woman and put a fierce, challenging glare upon Clay. "Who the hell are you; what business is this of yours?"

Clay kept his genial look as he answered. "Friend of the family, Mister, that's all. I heard the lady telling you she don't want to lease to you. That settles it, don't it?"

Sam's anger was solid now. He dropped his big right hand and straightened up to his full height. Behind him, those two rangeriders were stonily and intently watching their employer for the cue as to their own behaviour. The moment Sam's right arm straightened, both the cowboys eased up a little in their saddles and also became too relaxed, with their gun-arms hanging free.

Clay said, "Mister, don't do it. Don't make trouble."

Sam balanced a long moment before making his decision. He turned away and put his angry glare upon Agnes Cantrell. "All you ever had to do, Aggie, was *say* so, you didn't have to bring in no gunfighter." He turned on his spurred heel, clanked back down off the veranda, swung up across leather and whirled his horse.

Agnes turned, looking upwards. "It's been a busy morning, Mister Anderson."

Clay, still looking after the disappearing trio of rangemen, dropped his head and smiled at her. "Yes'm, it sure has." He started to move past. "I'd best go down and see to my horse."

She turned with him, and without a word walked along at his side through the thin, hanging dust stirred to life by the three rangemen who had so recently departed.

The sunshine was pleasant, the warmth was welcome, and he would not have denied that the beautiful woman at his side was also very welcome. He slowed his stride a little, and it therefore took them longer to reach the tie-rack and the barn, where he led his bay, to off-saddle it while Agnes crossed over to hold back a stall door for him, as she said, "Have you talked to Sam Waters before, Mister Anderson?"

"No Ma'am. Like I said, I was in a saloon in town last night. They was standing on my left, and I overheard their talk."

"Then I wonder why he called you a gunfighter, Mister Anderson?" She said it very sweetly, but the look in her dark eyes was appraising him as he led the bay over to the stall, and turned him in.

"Just talk, Ma'am, just something he said on the spur of the moment. He was mad, and I reckon he was also pretty darned surprised when I stepped out of the house to back you up." Clay turned, latched the door, then leaned upon it and steadily eyed her as he said, "You know something, Ma'am? You're prettier than your daughter." Now he straightened up to cross back and hang up his saddle, blanket and bridle.

She stared at him. Then she laughed, and went over where he was working. "Thank you, Mister Anderson. You know something? You're handsomer than Jack Barron."

He got tickled, for some reason, and loudly laughed, something he did not ordinarily do. He had a good sense of humour, he smiled often, and at times, when something truly amused him, he would laugh, but never loudly. Now, he laughed loudly.

She took him out back where the corrals were. They were old, most of the pole stringers sagged badly, and many of the posts had rotted in the ground and had been propped up. He said nothing about any of this, but it pained him to see it. Any stockman would have been pained to see how deterioration had taken over this ranch.

She leaned upon one large, round corral with some cattle in it, and said, "They don't look very good to you, do they, Mister Anderson?"

He looked in at the cows. They were large animals, broad hipped and deep-bellied; they were well-bred animals—but far too old. They did not have a bucketful of grinding teeth among the lot of them, but all he said was, "Fine breeding, Ma'am."

She turned. "But too old."

He hedged. "Maybe just a mite agey, Miz' Cantrell. But you could remedy that in a few years by holding back replacement heifers."

"No, Mister Anderson, not when you have to sell every single calf you raise to meet expenses, you can't hold back replacements." She turned, set her shoulders to the corral and gravely stood there looking far out. "If Sam had mentioned buying instead of leasing, I'd have listened, but leasing is no better than what Len and I've been doing since she first began to do our riding." The dark eyes swept around and upwards. "We've been holding our own, that's all."

Clay stared past at the big old cows, and after a moment, he turned to look out and around, in the same direction she'd been looking, as he said, "It's not just hang on or sink, Miz' Cantrell."

She got a faint scowl across her forehead. "That is exactly what it is, Mister Anderson."

He faced her. "Sure don't like arguing, but maybe I've got to this time." He waved a thick arm. "How many cattle do you have to run to live good, Ma'am, you got any idea?"

"Five hundred cows, and the bulls for them, Mister Anderson. I've figured that out."

He said, "In this kind of country, Ma'am, you could run five hundred and fifty head on a lot less land than you own. Sell down to just the range you need, then use the money to build up to five hundred and fifty head." He glanced around them. "Tear down those old pole corrals and build some decent ones—with a good chute. Make some holding pens and horse corrals." He looked at her, took down a breath and went whole-hog. "And get the damned place cleaned up and made workable." Then, having said all this, he grinned at her. "Sure sticking my beak in where it don't belong, aren't I? But I've been in this business all my life, and it bothers me to see a rundown cow outfit."

She gazed steadily at him for a moment longer before slowly turning to look southward, down across the glass-clear open country which ran more miles southward, westerly and easterly, than a person could ride in a week. Very gradually her glance became fixed in one particular direction, then she said, "I haven't seen that in twenty years, Mister Anderson," and he turned to follow out the way she was staring.

There was a rope-thin spiral of red smoke rising straight up into the stillness, and for it to be visible this far, Eusebio Gutierrez had had to heap on a great amount of faggots and greasewood.

Clay said nothing as he studied the smoke. The woman

beside him said, quietly, "That used to be the signal when Indians were raiding through the country. That red smoke."

He already knew this. "Lady, this time it isn't Indians. It's Jack Barron on his way out here." He looked down at her. "The Messican liverybarn-man in town agreed to signal like that when Jack come along."

She spoke swiftly, with a mother's foremost concern. "Len . . ."

Clay understood. "Just tell me where she'll be riding." He jerked his head and turned back towards the rear opening of the barn. "Come along."

She trailed him into the barn, where he led forth the bay and went to work rigging out. For a moment she watched without speaking, then she moved towards the harness-room and when she returned she was carrying an old sweat-stiffened leather carbine boot with a Winchester's butt jutting upwards. She handed it to him. "I don't think that gun's been fired in twenty years, Mister Anderson."

He believed her after he'd hauled the gun out to slide back the breach and look inside. The gun was covered with dust, but it was oily inside, and the dull brass casing that lay in the firing chamber looked perfectly serviceable. He slid the breach closed, rammed the gun back into the boot, then went to work buckling the scabbard into place under his fender, butt-forward, as he repeated his question.

"Where did Len ride to, Ma'am?"

Agnes was not sure because it was a large range and Len customarily covered a lot of it, when she was cow or horse hunting. "Probably southwest, Mister Anderson. There is an old adobe waterbox down there, near a spring. That's where our animals drink. But if she isn't there, she might be on the upper range, near Sam's line, because we very often have to push back his drift."

Clay looked down his nose at her. The girl was either miles southward or miles northward; that was like saying she was in heaven or hell, as far as he was concerned, but he smiled downward, confident that whether he found the girl or not, Len was not really in any serious jeopardy. Even if Jack Barron found Len before Clay did, there was one thing Clay was sure of—he was not going to make trouble, not for Lenore Cantrell. He was a lot more likely to make trouble for Clay Anderson.

He led the bay out into the sunshine, turned him once before mounting, and from the saddle he said, "Maybe he'll ride directly here, to the buildings. If he does, just tell him to set down and wait, that I'll be back directly."

She nodded. For a moment she said nothing, then she turned and very slowly walked back in the direction of the house.

TWELVE
THE ADVANCING DAY

THE COUNTRY was immense, visibility was excellent—but there was nothing to see, no movement at all—and one girl on a horse who could have been just about anywhere in her hunt for cattle, would have offered enough of a challenge to the burly man who went looking for her, even if he had known the lie of the land, which he didn't.

He had seen enough, from the rims the previous day, to respect its size, and to some extent, its wild, cow-country diversity. As for finding the girl—he anticipated no trouble at all.

He was no Indian, but the moment he picked up fresh shod-horse sign heading easterly, not north nor south as Agnes had suggested, he put the bay upon the trail and kept him on it, right or wrong.

The only other fresh sign had been made by three riders, not one solitary rider, and those three riders had struck out on an angling course which would eventually put them upon the range of Sam Waters.

He was not interested in those riders, he was interested in the other sign, the tracks leading eastward. In support of his feelings that this was the correct course was the knowledge that he had encountered a few little bands of those old Walking C cows in that direction, himself, earlier in the day. Len had said she was going cow-hunting.

When he was satisfied he could detect the sign, and was equally as satisfied he would find the girl, he lifted the bay over into a loose lope and let the horse rocket along on a loose rein while he sat up there examining the countryside in all directions, but mostly southward, and dead ahead.

He saw nothing, even when he was over far enough to catch sight of the stageroad—and that big old tree beside it which denoted the point of departure for the Cantrell range.

Far ahead, but looking much closer in the winy air, loomed those same forested slopes he had ventured over from Carleton's Meadow. They looked as darkly inhospitable even at this distance as he knew them to be.

Once, his attention was caught and held by a dust-flinging stage coming up from the direction of Las Cruces, and heading northward as straight as an arrow, its red body faded down to a rusty colour and its once-yellow wheels and running gear stained to the dun colour of the ground it had been traversing for so many years.

Then the coach hastened on up the roadway, and Clay saw a number of plodding cows come trooping up out of a swale, bags swinging, fat calves phlegmatically marching beside their mothers, the entire procession moving in the unmistakable manner that cattle moved when they were being driven.

He hauled down to a stop, leaned upon the saddlehorn and waited. When Len appeared, her horse ambling along as though none of this were the least bit interesting, Clay had to smile to himself. She rode as though she were as old as he was, as though she were as bored as he sometimes got, working the range, and working range cattle, the difference being that he'd been doing it since about the time she'd been born, and she was still quite young, whether she acted bored or not.

Then she saw him sitting out there and for a moment her rein-hand raised while her gun-hand dropped straight down. That tickled him too. She reacted as a man would have, not as a girl would be expected to react. He wagged his head and urged the bay ahead in an easy walk. The old cows eyed his advancing askance and gave way warily, then kept right on plodding.

The beautiful girl said, "What are you doing out here?" as soon as they were close enough to converse without shouting.

He was honest. "Looking for you. Jack Barron's on his way to the ranch."

This bit of information seemed to impress her a lot less than the fact that Clay had been able to track her. She eyed him in lively interest. "Mister Anderson, I've been thinking; why have you gone to all this trouble?"

He understood what she meant, and shrugged it off. "Just getting nosy in my old age," he said, and smiled at her. "As long as we're asking questions, maybe you wouldn't mind answering one for me. What is your opinion of Jack Barron?"

She looked ahead where the cattle were obediently hiking along, then she swung her head to look southward before answering him. "I liked him, that night of the dance; and that night out behind the barn, I could have shot him." She turned back. "I don't know what my opinion of him is, to be very truthful with you, Mister Anderson. I think—I still like him."

"And you wouldn't have shot him," murmured Clay. "Any more than he'd have shot you."

"Well, probably not. But he's an outlaw."

"Pshaw! I've seen horses come nearer to being outlaws than he's come. Maybe, if your paw had lived, or if you'd been a man instead of a woman, he might have done something rash—but those things didn't happen, did they?"

She cocked her head a little. "Mister Anderson, what exactly are you trying to do?"

"Keep a damned idiot from getting himself shot or hanged."

"Why? What do you owe Jack Barron?"

Clay raised a gloved hand to his jaw before answering, looking a little dubious about his own motives. "Owe him? Lenore, if anything it's the other way around. I owe him a kick in the britches, for the trouble he's caused me." He dropped the hand back to his saddlehorn and grinned over at her. "But I'll tell you a secret; him and me started out in life pretty much along the same lines. But I was a little luckier than he was; an old buffler hunter took me in when I was young and drifting, yanked the slack out of me every time I got bitter against things, and he also worked the hell out of me, gave me my first horse, my first pair of boots, my first saddle, and finally, when I was old enough to head out, he also gave me my first gun. Then he told me to work hard, which he taught me how to do, never to lie, never to steal, and maybe someday if I run across another young idiot like I was, to take him in hand, and in that way to work off the debt I owed the old buffler hunter."

She smiled. "I wish I'd known that buffalo hunter."

Clay nodded. "I wish you could have known him, too. But he's been gone a long while now. Anyway—that's my secret. That's what I'm doing now; working off an old debt." He laughed. "Even if it kills me."

They had the ranch in sight by this time, and the sun had made its high, curved crossing from east to west and was beginning to sink lower in the direction of the farthest ridges. Clay did not watch the cattle, which was just as well since the old cows had been brought to the home-place so often over the past fifteen or eighteen years they could have found it blindfolded, but he kept a sharp look upon the tree-shaded old buildings, looking for some sign of a saddled horse.

He did not see anything like this, but that did not have to mean much; any rider meaning to stay around for any length of time would have barned and stalled his animal.

He asked Len if she meant to corral the critters, and she answered him while also studying the yard, and tie-racks, up ahead. "No; I just wanted them closer to home. The feed's still long over here. In the spring and fall I like to have them where I can watch them calve-out."

He nodded, saying nothing but thinking to himself that those old cows had been calving without difficulty for so long now, they didn't need any watching.

He saw a man saunter to the doorway of the barn and stand there, thumbs hooked in his shellbelt, gazing out where the pair of horsemen were drifting in the band of critters, but the man's build was wrong for Jack Barron, was a hard and angular, lean and lithe individual.

He said, "There's a feller at the barn," to Len, and when she was looking in that direction, he also asked if she recognised the man.

She didn't, but she rode onward another dozen or so yards before being certain of this, and answering. "I thought it might be Sam, but I can see now that man is darker and younger, although he's built about like Mister Waters."

Clay had a sudden thought that Jack Barron had not come alone, and this idea was supported by his reflection that Jack probably rode over the rims, on Clay's trail, encountered those 'breeds up there, and had brought several of them along into the Las Cruces country with him.

This would complicate things, but perhaps Clay had made a misjudgement in assuming that Jack Barron would come alone, the way most men would have done. As they continued on closer to the yard, Lenore looked puzzled and finally said, "Who *is* he? It's not Jack, and it's no one from around here."

Clay was only a couple of hundred yards out when another man materialised, this time ambling up from the north side of the barn, evidently having been out back somewhere. Clay recognised this man at once. It was the cowman named Smith, Jess Smith, who had been with Sheriff Whit Mosely over at the old abandoned ranch, in the fog. Clay now turned and made a study of the man standing in the barn opening with his hands hooked in his shellbelt—and recognised him too, Sheriff Mosely!

Clay rode the balance of the intervening distance in silence. They may have just happened to be over here. They could just as easily have trailed Clay, although he doubted that they'd done that, or they might have captured Jack and brought him along as bait. One thing was sure enough, they did not have much reason to extend a cheery welcome to Clay Anderson.

The cattle turned northward to go up and around the yard. Clay and Lenore allowed them to do this, while they rode directly to the yard. Just before they were close enough to be heard, Clay said, "The feller in the doorway is Sheriff Mosely from over in the Tiburon country. That older man along the north corner is a cowman from over there named Jess Smith."

Lenore turned with a worried look, but she said nothing, and as they finally rode on over to the hitch-rack out front of the barn, Sheriff Mosely strolled ahead, still with both hands hooked in his gunbelt. He flicked a disinterested glance over Len, then turned his full, hostile attention towards Clay.

"Got a warrant for you," he said, antagonism as thick around him as it could be.

Clay dismounted, eyed the lawman, eyed Jess Smith who was now striding forward, too, then looped his reins and answered Mosely. "A warrant for what?"

"Bein' a fugitive from the law, that's for what!" snarled the lawman.

Clay looked harshly at Mosely. "What's the crime?" he demanded. "You never had a charge against me, not even when you tried to take me to your town. I was in the same barn with Jack Barron, and I wouldn't let you lynch him, that's all you ever had against me, Sheriff."

"You're goin' back with us," exclaimed Mosely.

Clay looked over where the grizzled cowman was standing, listening. Jess Smith had another sixgun in his holster. His original weapon was in the holster Clay was wearing. Smith returned Clay's flinty look, but said nothing, so Clay returned his attention to Mosely.

"Why me, Sheriff? Why not Barron—or couldn't you catch him?"

Mosely's lipless wound of a mouth pulled back wide

in a lethal smile. "I'll get him, Anderson. I heard down in Las Cruces that he was hereabouts. Me'n Jess was passing through on the southbound coach this morning when we also heard that you was hereabouts. Heard a Mex cafeman telling some fellers about a stranger who didn't know a word of Spanish, and he give your description. From there it wasn't hard figuring where you was. As Barron's riding partner, you'd be after the Cantrells too."

Clay shook his head. Mosely's rabid hatred might ordinarily have influenced him incorrectly, but this time, by a sheer fluke, it had done just the opposite. Mosely clinched this idea when he said, "We figured if you was here, Jack'd be close by. Anderson, you and the girl step inside the barn and we'll just sort of set down and wait."

Clay turned. Lenore was quizzically staring at Whit Mosely. Now, she said, "I'm going over to the house," and turned to walk off.

Mosely barked at her. "You get inside this damned barn, lady. Your maw's in there, and you'd better get in there too."

Lenore turned back, stared at Mosely, then reversed herself heading directly for the barn. It was nothing he had commanded her to do which had caused this abrupt reversal, Clay was sure of that; it was his announcement that Agnes was already in the barn that turned back her daughter, and a moment later when Sheriff Mosely ordered Clay inside, he obeyed, for the same reason.

As he moved past Jess Smith, the bitter-eyed cowman stepped in and lifted away the gun Clay was wearing. Clay turned and said, "It belongs to you, anyway."

The cowman grunted agreement, then herded Clay along while Whit Mosely went out to take charge of the saddled horses and hide them. When Jack Barron rode in, the yard, and the buildings, had to look as innocent and serene as possible.

THIRTEEN

A BAD SITUATION

LENORE WENT to her mother, who seemed to be quite calm despite the fact that she was being held a prisoner in her own barn. Agnes smiled at Clay, who wagged his head and ruefully smiled back, then he turned on the cowman with a remark.

"You just never seem to know when you're in bad company," he said.

Jess Smith was examining his retrieved sixgun. He ignored Clay's dig to ask a question. "How'd you get this weapon away from Jack?"

Clay answered truthfully. "Stole it, while he was asleep."

Mosely, tying the horses, looked up. "On Carleton's Meadow?" he asked.

Clay kept watching Jess Smith examining his sixgun.

"It's as good as when Jack yanked it off you," he told the cowman.

Mosely whirled in anger—he was not a man people could ignore with impunity, evidently. "Gawddamn you," he snarled at Clay. "When I ask, Mister, you'd better answer."

Clay turned his head and silently gazed at the irate lawman. "Yeah, I stole the gun off Jack at Carleton's Meadow. Now tell me, Sheriff, why didn't you come up there, when you could have nailed us both?"

Mosely snarled his retort. "You know damned well why not—the fog was so thick you couldn't make your way, that's why."

Clay continued to gaze at the lawman for a moment before turning back to the old cowman. "Mister Smith; did you ever run stock on Carleton's Meadow?"

The cowman nodded. "Yes. Several years—before the losses made me quit it."

"Then you know the fog don't reach up that high. I'd guess Sheriff Mosely'd know that, too. What I'd like to hear is what his *real* reason was, for not going up there after us."

The cowman shoved his retrieved Colt inside his waistband as he said, "Anderson, you're pushing for trouble. Why don't you just set back and wait until we're back over at the courthouse in Tiburon, then shoot off your mouth?"

"I'll tell you why," stated Clay, "because you're supportin' a bad choice of men, Mister Smith. I never broke any laws and I think you know that. But I *did* keep that louse over there with the horses from lynching a man, and for that he's after me any way he can get me, just like he's after Jack Barron because Jack ran off with a horse Mosely wanted. Mister Smith, you're in mighty bad company."

Mosely flung aside the tied reins of the black and the bay and started across the runway towards Clay. Both the cowman and Clay Anderson turned, facing him. Smith, who knew Mosely better than Clay could have, said, "Leave him be, Whit. Don't let him bait you into doing anything wrong. We just got to set here and wait. When Barron rides in, then we can head for home and get this damned mess over with."

Mosely halted, but he seemed willing to lunge at Clay even yet, except that Clay kept silent. Mosely then sneered, grunted his contempt, and returned to off-saddle the horses and stall them. There were two other stalled horses in the barn, the animals Mosely and Smith had got at the liverybarn in Las Cruces for the ride out to the Cantrell place.

Clay shoved back his hat, looked over where the women were, and ambled across to them looking disgusted. Agnes smiled softly up at him. "I had no idea who they were until the one with the badge herded me down here to the barn. He didn't say what he wanted until then, and I'm afraid I helped him. He said he was supposed to meet Jack Barron here, so I told him to sit down and wait, that Jack was coming. Then he drove me down here to the barn."

Clay involuntarily glanced out into the sunlit big yard, not because he expected to see Jack ride in, but because that thought was uppermost in his mind, and if he was any judge of men, Jack would react to the presence of the law the way any wanted man might react, and that, Clay was certain, was precisely what Whit Mosely of Tiburon wanted. He was seeking an excuse to kill an outlaw.

Lenore spoke out in a subdued tone to Clay. "He's rabid, Mister Anderson. He's dangerous."

Clay turned back and looked down into her white face. "Sure seems that way, don't it?" he drawled, then drifted his dark glance back to Agnes. She returned his steady regard with that same soft, gentle smile still across her face.

"You've done your best," she said.

He thought on that a moment before commenting. "I'm not quite through yet, Ma'am."

She reached and laid a hand upon his arm. He felt the cold hardness of steel through his sleeve and did not take his eyes off her face. She was still gently smiling, but her dark eyes were like steel, now. He very slowly raised his free hand to cover her fingers completely, and as she gently withdrew the hand, he felt the unmistakable shape of the under-and-over little big-bore derringer in his palm.

He pulled down a big breath, held it for as long as it took for him to fold his hand round the little gun and casually drop the hand to his left side, then he slowly let all his breath out, pocketed the belly-gun, and continued to stare at her. She murmured to him. "Women living alone, Mister Anderson, have to be defensive."

Over by the front of the barn Mosely and Smith were in solemn conversation. Mosely was profiled to Clay, while the cowman from time to time swung his head glancing back down where the captives were, and alternately glancing out and around the yard, and beyond it in the direction of Las Cruces. Smith seemed a lot less confident than Sheriff Mosely, but Clay had no illusions about the old cowman's sentiments. Jess Smith was one of those oldtime rangemen who tolerated book-law, and who lived according to range-law. Mosely, who represented book-law, had already proved to Clay's satisfaction back in the old Barron barn, that he too, lived according to range-law. He would have hanged Jack Barron in the old barn. Right now, he would not hesitate to shoot Clay Anderson, if he thought it were something which should be done.

In a sense, Sheriff Mosely was a paradox, a blend of the old and the new. He served the legal statutes, but he was also convinced of the rightness of the earlier laws. There were many lawmen like him on the frontier, even yet.

Clay left the women to saunter over, lean on the door of his bay horse, and look in. The big animal was picking through chaff and straw searching hopefully for a grain-head. He was entirely unconcerned with the difficulties of the two-legged creatures around him. Clay straightened up and glanced towards the front of the barn where Mosely and Smith were no longer conversing, but were standing loosely, keeping watch for the horseman they expected to ride into the yard any moment.

Clay shook his head, then sauntered up nearer the front opening. All his plans had come to nothing. He blamed himself, because if he hadn't lingered, once he'd got clear of Jack Barron, if he'd done what he'd been saying he was going to do—get the hell out of this New Mexico country and back up where he belonged—a young buck whose twisted motives and whose genuine feelings were so definitely different, would not now be riding straight into the gunbarrel of a lawman who meant to kill him. Clay had no illusions at all; Whit Mosely was going to shoot Jack Barron on sight, or as near to on-sight as he could do it, and still have it look like a justified killing.

When he reached the vicinity of the two men from Tiburon he ignored the lawman and spoke to Jess Smith. "Sure doesn't pay to try and do a good turn, does it?"

The cowman turned his hard, grizzled features. "You talking about the kid, Jack Barron?"

"Yeah."

"What good turn was you trying to do him?"

Clay glanced out into the sunlight. "Well. He struck me as being more misfit than mean, Mister Smith. I sort of had some idea he could maybe be yanked up short and set tight."

Mosely jeered at this. "How; by getting him over here to kill these women, Anderson? Who do you think you're fooling?"

Clay lay a scornful glance upon Mosely. "He's had ten years to kill 'em, Sheriff. Did he do it? In fact, he's had ten years to prove he's a killer, or even a genuine badman—has he done that either? Hell no. I've owned dogs that were meaner than Jack is."

Mosely's sneer remained fixed across his hard features. "You been in our territory what—one week?—and already you know how to judge the folks in it. I'll tell you what I think you are, Anderson—a damned fool, and along with that, a devious sort of underhanded carrion-hunter."

Clay allowed the lawman to finish without interrupting him. He allowed another few moments to pass after Mosely had had his say, before answering, and even then, although he had every right to show anger, he only showed contempt. "If I was all you say, Sheriff, I still wouldn't be as bad as you are. Standing there with a gun in your hand, waiting to kill Barron before he even knows you're over here. I figured you right back at the old barn—you're not a man, you're a lousy animal, a lousy wolf."

Mosely raised up to spring ahead, but Jess Smith was faster. He stepped squarely between them and growled at the lawman. "Hold up, damn it all. Whit, don't let him bait you. He ain't armed. You can't shoot him." Smith turned a fierce look upon Clay. "Damn you, anyway. You get back down there with the womenfolk."

Clay shrugged, but did not move until he'd said, "All right. But Mister Smith—he's using you. He's going to get you involved in a murder as sure as I'm a foot tall."

"Git!" snapped the cowman. "Go on down there, and keep your damned mouth shut, Anderson!"

Clay was turning away to obey, when from a considerable distance, a man's high shout rang down the hushed, warm afternoon, bringing everyone inside the barn straight up, listening.

Mosely blurted out his assessment. "That's Barron. He's halloing the house from southward, sure as hell. Jess . . . !"

"Calm down," growled the cowman, twisting to peer down across the yard in the direction of the main-house. "If he's coming inland from the stageroad, Whit, he'll come around the house."

"And by gawd we'll get him," stated the lawman, moving ahead, closer to the big barn doorway to look southward.

Smith turned, saw Clay, and gestured with his sixgun. "Go on. Do like I told you; and keep them women quiet."

Clay hesitated, but the cowman's sixgun was a strong influencing factor. Clay reluctantly went down where the women were standing together like carved statues. They had heard that high cry, and they had also witnessed the reaction of the men from Tiburon to it. Lenore reached for Clay's arm. Her fingernails dug into his flesh.

"They'll kill him," she gasped. "They don't intend to give him any chance at all."

Clay shook his head. "That's not Barron. That was a deeper voice. I'd say it belonged to an older man." He freed his arm from the painful fingernails and looked past at Agnes. She was concentrating on Clay Anderson, not on anything else. He leaned a little. "Is that derringer loaded, Ma'am?"

She nodded. "Both barrels. It is a forty-one calibre. Mister Anderson, you've got to be very close to hit anyone with it."

He already knew this. He would not only have to be very close, but he could not miss with either slug, because if he did, either Jess or Whit would kill him.

He slid his hand into the pocket where the little heavy gun lay, curled it into his hand, and turned to look up where Mosely and Smith had faded back out of sight from the yard on either side of the barn-opening.

FOURTEEN

A FIGHT FOR LIFE!

IT WAS a bad time for everyone inside the adobe barn, but it was hardest on the two women and Clay Anderson, while they all remained silent in the late day, waiting for whatever was to happen next.

Clay knew better than to walk back to the front of the barn. Those waiting armed men up there were in no mood to remonstrate with him again.

The only way he could hope to use the little gun Agnes Cantrell had slipped to him was to get up there. If he tried using it from the distance which now separated him from the cowman and Whit Mosely, they would kill him.

He had an additional cause for worry now, too. If the man who had let out that cry from southward, beyond the main-house, jogged into sight of the waiting armed men, and happened to resemble Jack Barron, he was going to ride to his death as sure as God made green apples, and maybe that would also be Clay's fault; it might also add to the burden his conscience was already carrying.

Jess Smith spoke to Mosely, cutting across Clay's thoughts. "What the hell's taking him so long?"

Mosely, straining around the huge fir upright on his side of the barn opening, did not reply, he simply leaned out for a better look, then he suddenly stiffened and pulled back as he hissed across to Smith.

"I heard him. He's coming. Now remember, Jess, you let me hail him—once."

Mosely turned to peer out, and Clay moved off to one side of the women to also look out into the yard, but there was no way for him to see southward as far as the house, so he started to face back—and a man suddenly appeared in the rear opening, far back, and saw Clay staring at him. The man threw up his Colt and yelled. Clay ducked. He did not wait to hear whatever the man had to say, he doubled down and rushed at the women, bowling them over and rolling them sideways.

The man's shout was muted inside the barn, but it carried amply far for the two hiding men up front to hear it and whirl. Clay did not understand the words, but he thought they ordered Mosely and Smith to throw down their weapons. Things happened too fast for anyone to be sure.

Jess Smith flung himself backwards and sideways, but before Mosely dropped and rolled, he fired at the man in the rear opening, and that man fired back, twice. Whoever he was, he was good with a Colt—those two shots sounded so close together the noise seemed to be a continuation; no small accomplishment when a man was firing a single-action sixgun.

Clay raised his head to look, but the stranger was no longer back there. Beyond, out in the fading sunlight black-powder smoke hung like dirty dust in the after-noon air, but there was no one visible out there at all.

Mosely shouted for Jess to watch the front opening as he got to his feet and charged towards the rear of the barn. When he passed Clay, Mosely's face was twisted by an expression of pure ferocity.

But that was all. There were no more shouts, no more gunshots; the silence returned and settled in thicker than ever. Finally, Jess Smith called back to Sheriff Mosely.

"That wasn't Jack. He was shorter and thicker. Who the hell was he?"

Mosely's answer was curt. "One of those gawddamned 'breeds Barron runs with."

That seemed to unsettle Jess Smith. "Whit, there's a lot of them 'breeds. Maybe he come down here with the whole pack. In that case we're in a bad . . . ."

"Shut up, gawddammit, Jess, and mind the yard out front." Mosely sidled close to look out back, but he never exposed his head to do this, and as he finally pulled back he had a little more to say. "Don't make a damned bit of difference how many he's brought with him, Jess. They're outside and we got all the protection we'll ever need."

Clay raised up slightly, saw that Lenore and her mother were sitting over against the front of a horse-stall. Agnes's dark eyes met Clay's glance. She slowly shook her head at him, then ruefully smiled. He did not smile back, but he kept looking at her because he'd never before seen a woman who acted as calm under conditions like these. She was quite a woman.

Clay pulled out the derringer, cupped it out of sight in his palm, and kept watching Sheriff Mosely. He might get a chance, after all, now that the pair of defenders were diverted enough not to be watching one another.

A man suddenly called out in a gruff-sounding, angry voice. "Whoever you are in the barn, this is the law. You walk out of there with your hands over your heads!"

Clay heard Jess Smith swear. He also saw Sheriff Mosely twist to glance up in Smith's direction. "The law hell," called Mosely. "That's Barron and his lousy half-breeds trying to bait us out of here so they can shoot us down. Jess . . . ?"

Smith looked down there, his face a study of doubt. "You sure of that, Whit?"

Mosely lied. "Damned right I'm sure. I *saw* him back here."

Clay knew this was not the truth. Sheriff Mosely had not poked his head out at all. Clay turned to call to Smith but that angry, gruff-sounding man outside spoke again.

"I'm not going to wait all day. You fellers pitch out your weapons, then march out of there, hands high. If you don't, by gawd, I'm going to come in there and yank you inside out!"

Mosely leaned, shoved out his right arm, fired, snagged back the hammer and fired again. He did that four times, until his gun was shot out, then he pulled back, set his shoulders to the thick adobe wall and went to work reloading while the furious attack he had incited raged out behind the barn, and up front, from the yard, where it seemed to Clay there were at least three more gunmen.

Clay wriggled over to the women, tried to over-shout the gunthunder, gave that up, got a stall door open and gestured for them to get inside where there would be more protection. They obeyed him, and afterwards, he partially closed the door, then settled his body in the opening so that he could see out.

There had to be at least five men attacking the barn, he told himself. If there were any less than that, then they were sure enough the gun-handiest crew he'd ever run across, because it would take either genuine gunfighters, or at least five ordinary men to keep up the firing that was now taking place.

If Jess Smith had entertained doubts before, he had no chance to voice them; all he could do was try and avoid being struck, by hiding around the sharp corner of the front opening, and occasionally poke his arm out to blind-fire, the way Mosely had done to start this fresh phase of the fight.

Mosely had his weapon reloaded, finally, and joined the fight. His additional gunfire seemed to anger the attackers anew. They burned lead into the barn, sluicing it from floor-height to hat-height, but always on an angle because it would have been suicide for any of them to try and get into position out back, or up front, to shoot directly down through the old barn.

It was this oblique gunfire that had endangered the women, and Clay Anderson. It did not endanger either Smith or Mosely, because it did not come anywhere near their positions, but the way it slanted inwards and all around, Clay could hear it striking into the walls, and even several of the stall-fronts.

Then the deafening sound stopped again, very abruptly, as it had done twice before. Clay, watching Sheriff Mosely, hoping to get his chance, saw the sheriff lean to plug out spent casings, then plug in fresh loads. He shook his head. Mosely was a madman. He had to be, to think he could come out of this unscathed.

But Clay kept silent. Mosely was keyed up to fire instantly at anything that moved or made a sound, and he was beyond accurate belly-gun range, so Clay would be unable to fire back with much hope of hitting his target.

Once more, that gruff-voiced man outside sang out. But this time he did not sound as though he wanted the besieged people to surrender. He said, "If you got the Cantrell womenfolk in there, let 'em come out. We don't want to hurt any bystanders." This was no offer to Mosely or Smith, and from the sound of the voice out there, there was not going to be any offer.

Mosely answered, for the first time. "You want the womenfolk? All right, you son of a bitch—you come in here and get 'em!"

Clay winced, expecting the gunfire to brisk up again. Instead, the angry man sounded a little less angry when he answered Mosely. "Mister, you're going to die in that gawddamned barn, but that's no reason to get the women hurt."

Mosely yelled back. "Where's Barron—you bastard?"

For a moment there was no reply. When it finally came, the anger had turned slightly to bewilderment. "You talking about *Jack* Barron?"

Mosely turned, looked up where Jess was leaning and listening, and said, "The underhanded son of a bitch. He's trying to gull us, Jess." Then he raised his voice and yelled back in a jeering fashion. "Yeah, that's exactly who I mean—Jack Barron. Jack? You hear me? This is Sheriff Mosely. You are not going to . . . !"

"What did you say?" roared the gruff-voiced man. "Who did you say you are?"

"Sheriff Whit Mosely from Tiburon, and you damned well know it, too, you skulking 'breed bastards."

There was a moment of breathless hush. Clay leaned to look up where Jess Smith had reloaded and was now standing with a little less resolution than before. Jess called down to Sheriff Mosely.

"I got a terrible feeling, Whit, we haven't been up against Barron at all."

"Like hell," jeered Mosely. "I know he's out there. I know what he's trying to do. Jess, you watch things up there; they're trying something sure as hell."

Clay turned when Agnes leaned and brushed his arm. She said, "That's Burt Meredith, Mister Anderson. He's the lawman down at Las Cruces. I'm sure of it, I've known Burt for fifteen years. I'd know his voice anywhere."

Clay leaned out, saw Mosely raising his gun and stealthily sidling ahead to risk a gunshot outside, and yelled at him. "Sheriff! That's the law from Las Cruces out there!"

Mosely stopped moving, turned only his head, and glared over where Clay was partially concealed. Clay eased up the little derringer scarcely breathing because he expected Mosely to whirl to fire.

Outside, the gruff man called out again. "Sheriff Mosely, you listening? This here is the law from Las Cruces. Sheriff Meredith. You hear me, Sheriff Mosely?"

Clay was fascinated at the change which gradually came over Whit Mosely. He was not relieved, he was infuriated. His face showed only murder.

Jess Smith yelled down to the lawman. "Whit, by gawd it's *not* Jack and his 'breeds."

Mosely spoke swiftly when he replied to the cowman. "I warned you, Jess. I told you it was Jack and he's trying to bait us out so's he can kill us. I *know* it's him!"

Agnes stirred and Clay swung to see what she was doing. Agnes was rising up to her feet to face Sheriff Mosely and refute what he'd just said. Clay grabbed and hauled hard to bring her back down, and to hold her down while he pushed his face close to warn her.

"Don't say a word. Don't let him see you." Clay did not explain, there was not sufficient time.

Meredith called to Mosely again. "Sheriff? If you were figuring to catch Jack Barron, take my word for it, he's nowhere hereabouts. This is just me and six posse-men from town. We heard from a Messican feller in Las Cruces there was something bad going on out here, so we rode out. Sheriff Mosely . . . ?"

Clay watched Jess Smith holster his weapon and start back down through, towards the rear of the barn, speaking to Whit Mosely as he paced along.

"That's not Jack Barron, Whit. Sure as hell that feller's telling the truth. Whit . . . ?"

Mosely turned, set his back to the thick rear wall and watched Smith coming towards him. Clay, with no idea what Mosely might do, raised the little derringer, took as good a rest as he could upon the chipped and cribbed boards of the horse-stall, and waited. If Mosely raised his weapon Clay was going to kill him, if he possibly could.

But Mosely did not raise the gun. It hung in his right hand at his side, even after Jess Smith got down there to say, "Call him in, Whit. If you don't, I will. We been fighting the law."

Mosely finally holstered his Colt and looked past, over where Clay was leaning, watching, then he said, "Call him in," to Jess Smith, and turned away.

Clay was fascinated by the lawman's behaviour. He had known from the beginning that Mosely was a killer, but he had not tried to anticipate how Mosely would have reacted under this kind of bizarre situation. Now, it seemed that Sheriff Mosely was beaten, was completely vanquished and demoralised. He walked along the rear barn wall and did not even turn when Jess Smith yelled out the back opening.

"Sheriff Meredith? This here is Jess Smith. I been in here with Whit Mosely. I'm not going to pitch out my gun to you—yet—but if you want to come in, neither one of us is going to raise a hand to stop you. Sheriff; we got two women in here—and an unarmed rangerider named Anderson. Sheriff—you coming?"

Meredith answered harshly. "Yeah, we're coming, and so help you if you got a gun in your hand, Mister Smith!"

Clay leaned back, twisted and saw the pair of white faces behind him. He said, "You ladies all right?"

Agnes answered. "I'll never understand why we didn't get hit, Mister Anderson."

He had to agree with her. He did not say so aloud, but he had to agree with her. There had been enough lead buzzing round inside the old barn to make it seem like the inside of a hornet's nest. Probably, the main reason none of them had been hit was that bullets did not ricochet off adobe, they either drove right on in, or they flattened against it, tearing out hand-sized chunks. Another major reason may have been that, aside from being protected inside the horse stall, the bullets had not driven directly at anything, they had simply been fired at random.

But it was still a miracle, and Clay had no illusions about that.

FIFTEEN
UNDER A BLOOD RED SUN

BURT MEREDITH, who had been so candidly described to Clay Anderson by the Mexican liveryman in Las Cruces, was a man of medium height, compactly put together, with features which under normal conditions could have been described as pleasant. But these were hardly normal conditions. When Sheriff Meredith came into the barn, with three of his possemen, while another three possemen appeared out front in the yard, none of them looked pleasant, but Sheriff Meredith looked the least pleasant.

Clay pocketed the little belly-gun, helped the women to their feet, watched as they dusted themselves off, then did the same to his trousers before turning and leaning in enormous relief upon the stall-front, watching Sheriff Meredith approach.

Whit Mosely and Jess Smith had holstered their weapons. Mosely was still acting oddly. At least it seemed that way to Clay Anderson.

Meredith, seeing the women, angled over in their direction to ask if they were all right. Agnes's eyes ironically shone. "Frightened out of my wits," she replied. "Otherwise we're all right, Burt." She turned. "Burt, this is Clay Anderson."

Meredith shook Clay's hand. "How'd you happen to be in here?" he asked, and this question brought Whit Mosely suddenly to life. He began exclaiming while he turned to stamp over to them.

"He's a fugitive from the law. I've got a warrant for him, and he's a running-mate with Jack Barron."

As he made this pronouncement, Mosely halted back a yard or so, and put his murderous stare upon Clay. He was projecting the impression of triumph. No matter what else had happened, Mosely still had Clay Anderson. He seemed willing to settle for that, although earlier he'd practically ignored Clay altogether, continually to speak of Jack Barron.

Sheriff Meredith put a stare of frank curiosity upon Whit Mosely. Obviously they had never before met. The five tough-looking rangemen whom Meredith had recruited to ride north with him from Las Cruces were also interested in Sheriff Mosely. One of them said, "Say, Sheriff, why in hell didn't you slack off when Burt told you who we was?"

It had been asked innocently enough, although there certainly was no mistaking the complaining tone.

Mosely's reaction was rage. He swung towards the posseman with a savage retort, and with his right hand upon the saw-handle grip of his holstered Colt.

"Why should I have believed you? I was searching for two fugitives and I had one. Therefore the other one had to be close by. Why should I believe there were any other lawmen anywhere around? You damned fool, if you were something besides a common rangeman, you'd understand."

"Whoa," said Burt Meredith, frowning at Mosely. "It was a perfectly fair question. I was fixing to ask it myself. And there's another thing, Sheriff Mosely . . ."

The Tiburon lawman made a chopping gesture with one arm. "It's over and done with. It was a mistake on my part, and Sheriff Meredith, it was a stupid thing to do, on your part, to jump into the rear doorway and yell for us to throw down our guns. But it's done, and now I'll take my prisoner back to Tiburon. Maybe, on the way, I'll find his running mate." Mosely looked up, smiling. "And if I do—don't you boys worry, you'll never have another worry about Jack Barron."

Clay was prepared to resist, but he was interested in the look on Sheriff Meredith's face, upon the face of Jess Smith, and upon one or two of the other faces standing there in the late-day, slanted sunlight.

Lenore and her mother were also staring steadily at Whitney Mosely. He did not seem to notice. In fact his attitude changed subtly, he smiled, he no longer seemed on the verge of furiously cursing, or of heaping blame on the other men, or of staring murderously at Clay Anderson.

He lifted his hat, swiped sweat from his forehead with a soiled sleeve, lowered the hat and strolled to the stall of the door holding his livery horse. He turned and said, "Let's get rigged out, Jess, and head for home."

Sheriff Meredith exchanged a glance with Jess, then said, "Sheriff, you won't get very far before nightfall. Why not come down to Las Cruces with us fellers and we'll put you up so's you can get an early start in the morning."

Mosely acted as though he had not heard. He turned, vacantly smiling at Jess. "Better shake a leg."

Clay finally left his place and moved over beside Sheriff Meredith. He leaned and whispered, "You'd better disarm him. I don't know what's gone wrong with him, but something sure as hell has."

Somewhere outside, sounding as though it came from the northeast, a horse blew its nose with considerable force, and for a moment or two no one paid much heed to that, until Lenore turned to pace towards the front of the barn. She, alone of everyone inside the adobe barn, knew there could be no horses up there, northeast of the yard, unless this particular horse was being ridden. She leaned, looked out, and Clay, who was looking after her, saw the way her body suddenly stiffened and her shoulders pulled back square in the reddening light of a dying day.

The men around Clay had heard the noise, but their interest was temporarily diverted when Sheriff Mosely opened the stall door of his livery animal and spoke as he went inside.

"Maybe the next time I'm over this way, I'll lie over and see the sights, but right now I got to get my prisoner back. If I find Barron on the trail . . . I almost got him once, but that's water under the bridge, I'll sure as hell hang the bastard yet."

Clay started to walk away, in the same direction Lenore had taken, but he did not get very far before he— and everyone else inside the barn—heard her call to someone.

"Get away from here! *Run for it, John!*"

Two of Meredith's rangerider-possemen turned to crane outward, but all they could actually see was Lenore. The man she had cried out so desperately to was not within sight. The possemen started forward. Clay was already two-thirds of the way to the doorway, and he got out there first, just in time to see the rider haul his dark horse to a sudden stop, staring at Lenore. Clay saw Jack Barron face to face over a fair distance, recognising him at once. He raised an arm fiercely to gesture.

"Do like she says," he called. "Get the hell away from here!"

Barron reacted instantly. He whirled his horse and sank in the spurs. He twisted in the saddle to glance over his shoulder as those two possemen charged forth from the barn. Clay spun to face the possemen, but neither of them did anything other than stand there staring after the furiously retreating rider.

Inside the barn, though, Sheriff Mosely had heard that calling, and had surmised its purpose. He started forward out of the stall grabbing for his belt-gun, his relaxed face of moments earlier becoming once more a twisted mask of unreasoning fury.

Jess Smith lunged to try and grab him, but he was too distant. So were Burt Meredith and another of his possemen who also lunged.

Clay, already looking back in the direction of the pair of stationary possemen, caught sight of that furious rush as Whit Mosely charged from the barn, and jumped squarely ahead blocking the lawman's path. He saw the gun coming up, and tried to swing his body sideways at the same moment that he made a desperate effort to lash out with his right arm. He did not make a solid contact, but he managed to brush Mosely and push him off stride as Mosely fired. The bullet ploughed hardpan-earth a hundred feet ahead. It endangered no one, least of all Jack Barron who was already a quarter of a mile away, northward, and widening the gap with each jump of his spurred horse, but Mosely, reverting again to his earlier ferocity, caught his balance and whirled on Clay Anderson, one thumb-pad hooked hard over the hammer as he turned, drawing back the hammer for his next shot.

A cowboy hurled himself awkwardly sideways and

bumped the lawman, but Mosely twisted from the waist to fire as Clay frantically dug in bootheels to jerk clear. This time the bullet ranged higher, and Clay felt it pull him as he dug for the little derringer. He felt nothing, no pain, no shock, but in the split second afterwards his mind registered the fact that he had not escaped. He dropped down, pulling out the little under-and-over gun with its three inch barrels, saw Mosely, saw four men converging on him, and saw the thick thumb hauling back the hammer for Mosely's next shot. Everything registered vividly, more clearly in fact than most things registered normally in his awareness.

He only had seconds. He did not try to raise his right hand, he only tipped it up as he cocked the derringer. Mosely's Colt was coming downward in a fast, chopping movement, when Clay fired.

The little derringer kicked harder than a larger handgun would have. It also made a noise as loud as a larger weapon. Clay desperately pulled the hammer back for the second and last shot, when Mosely fired.

This time, the lawman's bullet had a stationary target, but perhaps because Clay was lower to the ground than the gunman was, his bullet, which would normally have caught Clay Anderson in the midriff, or possibly a little higher, in the lower chest, gouged a bloody swath alongside Clay's head. As Anderson went sidewards and backwards from impact, already losing consciousness, his muscles reacted to the shock spasmodically and he fired off the last round from the lower barrel of the belly-gun.

There seemed to be a howling wind in the encompassing blackness that Clay was falling down through. He had no sensation of anything else, of crumpling at the feet of the astonished possemen, of the cry of Agnes, or even of the sensation of stunning pain that should have accompanied that head-shot.

For a moment everyone seemed rooted. All eyes were on Sheriff Mosely, who let his gun-hand sag back to his side as he looked down with an expression of incredulity across his strong, dark features. The spreading red stain high upon his shirt-front seeped slowly. It was the only wound but it was in a bad place. No one said a word, not even Sheriff Meredith whose outrage of a moment earlier, had turned to shock and horror as he had seen Clay go down, the side of his head turning scarlet, then, when Meredith looked up, he also saw the blood spreading across the upper body of Sheriff Mosely.

Agnes finally moved, she went over beside Clay and sank down. That was when Whit Mosely raised his face, looking steadily at Jess Smith, then let go all at once. His knees turned loose, springing outwards. He dropped his Colt and fell gently.

Someone whispered "Gawd-a'mighty," saying it so softly that normally it would have gone unnoticed, but there was not a sound until after this had been said, when Lenore turned to cross to her mother's side. At the same time Burt Meredith holstered his Colt and stepped round the pair of kneeling women to lean and gently ease Mosely over onto his back.

Jess Smith, standing close, said, "Dead, by gawd."

They turned back towards Clay. Agnes sent her daughter to the house on the run. With the same initiative she arose and, pointing, gave the men an order. "Lift him, please, and carry him over to the house."

Sheriff Meredith and Jess Smith stooped down to obey. Jess, closest to the hanging head, pursed his lips, waited until more men had taken hold to help at the carrying, then he said, "A half inch more and it would have tore loose half his skull."

Two men remained at the barn with dead Sheriff Mosely. They talked together, briefly, then one struck off to bring in the posse's horses. The man who remained behind rolled a cigarette, shoved back his hat and perched upon an up-ended horseshoe keg to sit and impassively study the dead lawman. Whatever it was that had motivated Whitney Mosely would probably not be clearly defined in the lifetime of any of the men—or women—who had witnessed his death, but one thing was clear: none of those witnesses would ever forget what had happened.

Outside, the sun was turning steadily redder, there were long shadows in all directions, cast earthward by the shaggy old ranch-yard trees, the hush had returned, and except for that dead man lying face up out front of the barn, the serenity could have been as it had always been, at least for the past twenty or so years, at the Cantrell ranch.

The smell of burnt black-powder was still strong, but it would eventually dissipate. There were bullet marks, too, mostly inside the adobe barn where they were not generally visible, and they would remain for as long as the old barn stood. They were the least significant factors which had gone into the making of this savage, and deadly, afternoon, and ironically they would last the longest.

SIXTEEN
A LONG NIGHT BEGINS

CLAY'S INJURY looked much worse than it was. By the time Sheriff Meredith and his possemen had to return to Las Cruces the night was well down, the stars were bright overhead, and the heat of the autumn afternoon had faded considerably, something it did not do in the summertime when the departure of the sun simply meant no direct sunlight but the heat remained.

Agnes went out to the veranda with Burt Meredith, looking as tired as she felt. Meredith said he would take the corpse of Tiburon's lawman back to town with him, have it preserved, crated, and sent to Tiburon by special coach first thing in the morning. He then asked if Agnes wanted him to take the Tiburon cowman, Jess Smith, back to Las Cruces too, and Agnes raised dark eyes in enquiry.

"Is he under arrest, Burt?"

Meredith considered a moment before replying. "No, I reckon not, Agnes, but he fired on a lawman, and that's . . ."

"Burt, *he* was the one inside the barn who was trying to make Sheriff Mosely stop shooting at you. He was the one who said they were fighting the law, not Jack Barron."

Meredith's earlier thought was not very strong, evidently, because now he said, "Well; I expect he wasn't too much at fault. But maybe you'd just as soon he wasn't left out here, after we're gone, Aggie."

She smiled. "My impression of Mister Smith is that he is a decent man, Burt." She laid a hand upon his arm. "I'll never be able to thank you properly for arriving when you did."

Sheriff Meredith thought a moment, then said, "Sure you can, Aggie. All you got to do is cook up a barbecue someday, and invite me," then, before she could reply to this, Meredith poked his head inside and called to his possemen. Afterwards, he waved to Agnes as he led the exodus in the direction of the barn.

Agnes returned to the bedroom where Jess Smith was leaning at a window in the rear wall, gazing out into the pleasant, quiet night. He turned, as did Lenore, when she walked in, but none of them spoke.

Clay's bandage made his face look even more lop-sided. It was bad enough without the bandage because most of the swelling and all the discolouration were on the same side. Jess Smith, looking over and watching Agnes as she leaned to use a damp cloth to wipe the unconscious man's hot-looking puffy face, said, "Has Meredith gone, Ma'am?"

Agnes replied without glancing up. "Yes, Mister Smith. He took Sheriff Mosely's body along to be taken care of in Las Cruces, then sent over to Tiburon by special stage." She looked up, slowly. "Did you want to go with them?"

Jess stepped clear of the window and went to a chair. Lenore, cutting fresh bandages nearby, ignored the old cowman but shot her mother a look, just as Smith said, "I don't know exactly what I'd ought to do, Miz' Cantrell. Going back with Sheriff Mosely's body might be the correct thing." He looked over at her. "But I'll tell you, Ma'am, while I was in your barn with him—it sort of come over me that what I'd figured was being a good lawman, plain *wasn't*. And I don't just mean what happened out there today, I mean—a lot of other things lately." He jutted his jaw in Clay's direction. "That feller stopped Whit from hanging Jack Barron. Right then, at that time, I didn't think it was plumb wrong. But later, it come to me—Whit and I wasn't Barron's judges, not really . . . And this afternoon . . ." Jess shook his head slowly, like a baffled old badger. "Something was plumb wrong, in there . . . No, I don't think I'll ride back with Whit's body."

Lenore went out to the kitchen to make a meal for her mother, herself, and Jess Smith. While she was gone, the older people sat quietly, only occasionally speaking, keeping a vigil, and just when Jess Smith's premonitions prompted him to say, "We'd ought to hunt up a doctor," Clay opened his eyes.

They did not see him do this; there were only two kerosene lamps in the bedroom, one at bedside, the other one across the room upon a high old oaken dresser. His eyes aimlessly rolled and as though from a considerable distance, he heard an occasional voice, belonging first to a woman, then to a man. He had a headache the like of which he had never even imagined. His eyes watered copiously, and his entire body ached.

He had been shot, he realised that, and in fragments, as he lay there trying to concentrate, it came back to him a little at a time. He heard someone enter the room, and looked down his nose to see Lenore. She was looking directly at him, from her full height, and was the first of them to notice that he had regained consciousness. Without saying a word to the old cowman or her mother, Lenore came to the bedside, leaned, studied his face a moment, then picked up what appeared to be a glass of water from the bedside table and held it for him to drink.

The water was as bitter as original sin. He got down

four swallows before he stopped, screwing up his face. Lenore smiled down at him. "You'll feel better in a few minutes."

It was the truth, and to Clay Anderson, it was also some kind of a miracle. He had no idea what laudanum tasted like, having never tasted it before, although he knew what it was.

Agnes held one of his hands in both of her hands and stood alongside the bed saying nothing. It was Jess Smith, from the foot of the bed, who spoke directly to Clay, and, man-like, he ignored the surroundings and Clay's condition to state facts.

"Mosely's dead, Mister Anderson. The law from Las Cruces has went back. You and me are all that's left around here, except for the womenfolk, and as far as I know, there's nothing against you . . . I'm sorry Whit shot you. It'll leave quite a scar up alongside your head. But at least you're better off than Whit is."

Having pronounced the barest facts, Jess Smith leaned a little on the foot of the bed, expecting Clay to respond, but all he got was a watery look.

Lenore slipped out of the room and did not return until the laudanum had taken full effect, then, when she came back with a bowl of broth, Clay was able to sit up and eat. He probably should not have been hungry, but he was. Agnes went to re-fill the bowl. While she was gone Clay finally spoke to Jess Smith.

"I reckon this'll be the best time for me to say this," he

told the cowman, "seeing as how you can't shoot a sick man . . . Mister Smith, you're one hell of a lousy judge of men."

Smith solemnly inclined his head, not the least bit indignant. "Sure does seem like it," he averred. Then he smiled. It was the first time Clay had ever seen him do this. "But maybe it's not just poor judgement, Mister Anderson, maybe it's something else."

"What, then?"

"Well; I'd have helped hang Jack Barron at the barn. I've leaned on a few ropes in my time. Maybe it's not bad judgement, but changing times that us older fellers have so much trouble handling."

Clay thought about that, then nodded his head. "Maybe. Mister Smith—years back a feller stole a horse from you."

The cowman nodded again, gravely. "Yeah. Odd thing about that, Mister Anderson. I didn't know it. Not at that time. Of course I had a lot of horses in those days. Sixty to seventy head, in fact, and losing one didn't mean anything. As for the young buck who stole it—well—if he'd come around and *asked,* I'd have given him the damned horse . . . And if you're leadin' up to me pressing charges, in the first place it was too long ago, I couldn't even describe the horse, in the second place, the hell with it."

Clay sighed. "I'm obliged, and if Jack had a lick of sense he'd be even more obliged. Now that brings me to the next thing. Four hundred dollars the damned fool took off a bullion coach a few years back."

Jess Smith straightened up off the foot of the bed and went to a chair to sit down. "I remember that. Remember it real well, in fact." He put a steady, narrow look back at the man on the bed. "At the time I was interested in the stage company. Hadn't yet bought in, but I was thinking about it when the coach got robbed. I bought in later that summer. We put up a hundred dollars reward, which wasn't much, and no one ever put in for it anyway."

"Suppose," said Clay, " I was to give you four hundred dollars, Mister Smith."

The cowman's narrowed eyes widened slightly. "You? Why should you do that?"

"To clear the damned fool that robbed your coach."

"What's he to you, Mister Anderson?"

"Well, up until I got this gouge alongside my head, he was just a damned idiot who isn't mean as much as he's sort of troubled by things he can't change, and which he'd do better plumb to forget. But now that I'm going to be scarred because I had in mind getting him to set on a straight trail, why I figure I got a personal stake in things. Do you want the four hundred dollars?"

Jess Smith leaned back in the chair, crossed his legs and sombrely studied the scuffed toe of one boot for a while before answering. "All right, Mister Anderson, I'll take it for the company. But that won't clear Jack with the law." Smith raised his head a little and stared at Clay. "But I'll tell you what I'll do. I'll talk to my brother."

Clay said, "That'll be nice. Is your brother with the stage outfit too?"

"No. He's the Executive Assistant to the Governor of New Mexico Territory."

Clay blinked. "The hell he is."

Jess ignored that. "He can get Jack pardoned, if full restitution is made, and no one presses charges. He's done it before." Jess sighed. "Jack went and stoled a black horse from the liverybarn over in Tiburon too, you know. Or didn't he tell you that?"

"Yeah, he told me. You don't happen to have another brother—who runs that liverybarn, do you, Mister Smith?"

The cowman's craggy face showed a hint of amusement. "No sir. I only got one brother. But the liveryman and I been friends forty years. In fact, I sort of helped him get started up in the livery business, back in those days when I run a lot of saddle stock. I think he'll listen . . . Mister Anderson, you could damned well be doing all this for nothing. You know that, don't you?"

Clay did not believe it for one moment. He did not have an opportunity to say this, though, because Agnes returned with more broth, and a cup of black coffee that sent its delicious aroma throughout the room. The moment Clay tasted that coffee, he looked at Agnes and smiled. It was liberally laced with rye whiskey. "You sure know what a man likes," he told her.

She stood a moment without speaking, then leaned to adjust the pair of pillows behind Clay and murmured. "You need rest, Mister Anderson. Finish the coffee and broth and lie back."

He finished the coffee but dawdled so long over the broth that eventually Agnes invited Jess Smith to go out to the kitchen for something to eat, and as soon as the cowman had departed, she leaned close and said, "You've got to rest. In the morning you'll want to feel better."

He couldn't argue with that, so he finished the broth, watched her remove the bowl, and when she turned to face him, he said, "You got any idea how old I am, Miz' Cantrell?"

She showed surprise. "How old you are? Why, no, and what difference could that make?"

"Maybe a lot. What I was going to tell you was that I never saw a woman before, in all those years, who really stacked up as good as a man."

She gazed at him a moment, then laughed, and moved briskly to wrap him, boots and all, in several blankets and a quilted comforter. As she stepped back and critically examined her work she said, "That was quite a compliment, Mister Anderson."

"It wasn't meant to be a compliment, Miz' Cantrell. It's the plain truth."

"That makes it even more of a compliment." She blew

down the lamp mantles then went to the door and smiled back at him. "You sleep, but if you need anything, call out. I'll be in the next room."

He said, "Good night," and closed his eyes, until she had departed, leaving his door cracked open just a tad, then he rolled back the covers, sat up and tugged off his boots, removed his gunbelt, scratched his chest for good measure, and the last thing he did—the last thing he had been doing for about three years now—was reach beneath his shirt and make certain the money-belt buckled round him, next to his hide, was still in place. It was.

He finally lay back, staring into the darkness, thinking that, hell, he never would have used that money to buy himself a piece of cow country anyway. Then he went to sleep.

SEVENTEEN
CLAY'S FINAL DECISION

HE DID not feel a whole lot better in the morning, but he felt a *little* better. At least the headache only bothered him when he sat up, or otherwise moved his head, as when he eased up off the bed and tugged on his boots. Otherwise, he felt shaky in the limbs.

It was very early, the sun was not yet up although the sky was beginning to change from purple to fish-belly grey when he stepped to the window and glanced out.

There was a drowsing horse at the tie-rack down in front of the barn.

He stared, felt uneasy and went over to pick up his gun and shellbelt and buckle them round his middle. The horse certainly hadn't been left like that all night, which meant there was a visitor somewhere around, before anyone was up.

He opened the door soundlessly and stepped into the short, dark corridor. There was not a sound, anywhere, until he tip-toed towards the parlour, then he vaguely heard a voice, and after a moment, a second voice. He palmed the sixgun, rested a thumb-pad atop the hammer and tip-toed across the dark, empty parlour, saw the orange reflection of lamplight under a door, and, raising the gun slightly, he went ahead, pushed the door open, and winced when lamplight hit his eyes.

The kitchen was warm, smelled of coffee, and two men at the table looked up, looked at the gun in his hand, then sat like stone until he'd pushed all the way through. Then Jess Smith said, "You don't look any better, Mister Anderson, but you sure must feel better. No need for that gun."

Jess reached for the big old graniteware coffee pot and growled at the younger man across the table from him. "Jack, fetch another cup. They're in the cupboard behind you."

Clay closed the door at his back, watched Jack Barron

go after the cup, slowly put up his weapon and slowly went over to sit down at the table. When Jack returned, Jess filled the cup and they shoved it in front of Clay, who put a steady, blood-shot stare upon the younger man.

"Is that your horse out yonder in front of the barn?" he asked, and when Jack said it was, Clay growled at him. "That's no way to treat an animal. You get out there and put him up proper, in the barn. And fork him some feed, too."

For a moment Jack Barron sat still, then he abruptly arose and without a word walked out of the room.

Jess cleared his throat, considered his work-scarred hands atop the table for a time, then spoke. "I come out for a drink of water an hour back. He was here, drinking coffee, with the girl. I sent her off to bed."

"What were they talking about?" Clay asked, picking up his cup.

"Them. They was talking about them two. He'd have to be a damned fool not to be sweet on her."

Clay felt better the minute the black coffee went down his gullet. He put down the cup and reached to adjust his slightly askew big head-wrap. "She likes him. I figured that out yesterday."

Jess said, "She'd be good for him, Mister Anderson."

Clay thought about that, but did not comment on it. Instead he said, "Mister Smith, I'm getting tired of being Mister Anderson so much."

The cowman accepted this. "Does for a fact make a man feel a lot older, don't it? Well . . . ?"

"Well, what?"

"Well, you've settled up the old scores for him. I told him that. And I told him if he had one lick of manliness to him, he'd work off that debt over the next fifty, sixty years."

"What did he say, Mister Smith?"

The cowman looked thoughtfully at Clay. "Are you trying to make me feel old?"

Clay grunted and leaned upon the tabletop. "No." Then he re-phrased the question. "What did he say, Jess?"

"He said I was exactly right."

Clay sighed and sat a moment in contemplation of his cup, then lifted it, drained off the last of the coffee and set the cup aside as he fished around for his tobacco sack.

Jess Smith watched the strong fingers curl up the cigarette. "I need a rangeboss," he said, suddenly. "I run eight hundred cows and I got no idea how many horses, and I'm getting—not too old, mind you—just getting to the place where I'd like to go up to Denver and out to San Francisco, now and then. You wouldn't be interested, would you?"

Clay blew smoke at the ceiling, then fell to studying the burning small red tip of his smoke. "Yes, I'd be interested—only I got a thought in mind, Jess."

The older man accepted this, and proved himself a person of perspicacity. "Right here, on the Cantrell place?"

Clay nodded. "It sure needs a man, Jess."

"That's a damned fact," assented the cowman, and cleared his throat. "Last night, Miz' Cantrell and I sat out here and talked a little before turning in."

Clay looked up, moving just his eyes.

"She wants you to stay," said Jess. "She's going to ask you about that in the morning. Only you don't have to tell her I told you any of this."

Clay pushed out his cigarette in a tin tray, eased back in the chair, reached up to be sure his bandage hadn't slipped again, and glanced out a shiny window where the fish-belly world was turning a different colour, was changing away from grey to a very delicate shade of blue. *This* part of New Mexico was not too different from some parts of Colorado and Montana he'd been in. It lacked all those criss-crossing big mountains Wyoming had, but mountains were not much good to a cowman, at least they were not as good as grass-country and around Las Cruces, at least around this part of the country-side around Las Cruces, there was plenty of grassland.

Jess Smith cut across his wandering thoughts. "I got to thinking, last night, after the lady and I'd been talking. If you took up her offer to stay on—well—from what I've seen of this country around her ranch, there's an awful lot of feed."

Clay brought his attention back to Jess Smith with a little effort, piqued at what the cowman was saying.

"The thing she needs here is cows. Not old gummer-cows, good, big-bellied, young cows." Jess looked steadily at Clay. "I'd guess she don't have the money to stock up, or she'd have done it. Well; you stay on with her, and I'll trail you over two hundred head, and she can pay me off out of the first four or five calf-crops. All right?"

Clay and old Jess looked steadily at one another for a moment, then Clay shoved out a hand. As they gripped, shook, and let go, Clay said, "Len'll do for a range-boss—and Jack sure as hell better work out as the rider."

Jess's lipless, tough mouth turned slightly upwards. "I expect, before you settle that, Clay, you'd better get it all threshed out with the lady." He arose, yawned, and turned towards the door. "I'll go see about the horses. When she comes along, directly now, you tell her."

Clay nodded, watched Jess leave the kitchen, and reached to re-fill his cup from the graniteware coffeepot. Hell; now he'd *never* get back to Montana. He put the cup aside, raised his eyes, and saw Agnes standing in the doorway looking completely surprised because he was sitting over there smiling. She looked as pretty as a spotted pony, and he already knew she was a damned good man.

Center Point Publishing
600 Brooks Road • PO Box 1
Thorndike ME 04986-0001 USA

(207) 568-3717

US & Canada:
1 800 929-9108